…to be made whole again.

By: Richard A. Rice, PE

DEDICATION

To God, and his son Jesus Christ

To my wife Barbara. Without her, I would be nothing, I would have nothing, and there would be nothing. She is everything.

To my daughters Suzanne and Jaclyn. My pride.

To all my friends who put up with me anyway.

CONTENTS

ACKNOWLEDGMENTS

Dr. Peter S. Parsonson, PhD, PE: Thank you for being my counselor, mentor and friend.

Chief Judge John C. Carbo, III: Thank you for the legal advice. Thank you and Linda for being such good friends to my family. And thank you for being a pretty good Sunday school teacher.

Flory Pulliam: Copy Editor - That you were able to put up with my grammatical buffoonery still amazes me.

Jeff Shropshire, vice-President
Roadway Division - C.W. Matthews Contracting Co., Inc.
Thank you for your help and advice. You are one of the good ones.
HFF

1 - A DOCTOR AND HER MENTOR

In 1992, Dr. Christine Dee Jesup celebrated her thirtieth birthday. This was also a year that would change her life forever. As a general practitioner and the "go-to" doctor for difficult deliveries, she was considered a near-saint by most of the people in the Low Country community of Sheldon, South Carolina. Christine was a local girl who was different than most other girls because of her desire to become a medical doctor. She was a caring person; perhaps because in losing her mother when she was just a baby, she could better sympathize with others in distress. During her high school years in the late 1970's, girls were discouraged from leaving the Low Country to become educated. While not openly discussed in polite company, girls were expected to marry young and to produce babies. When Christine was a young girl, she saw how the lack of medical services caused avoidable harm and sometimes, death. As a farmer's daughter (her daddy's name was Jack), she saw how his livestock often got better treatment than her human neighbors. She understood that the animals needed attention; but she resented it just the same.

Although far from unattractive, Christine did not possess the superficial beauty that was most appreciated in her high school years. That kind of appreciation was given to those on the cheerleading squad. Though she was taller than most girls her age, with brown hair and eyes, Christine's real beauty lay in her servant's heart. When not practicing or performing with her clarinet in the Beaufort High School Band, she participated in 4-H (an expected activity of a farmer's daughter), the Beta Club (as one of smartest people in her school), and, all through high school, as a candy striper at the Beaufort Memorial Hospital in the city of Beaufort.

ooooo

For many years, Dr. Maurice Honeycutt was the only physician at Beaufort Memorial by virtue of attrition. He graduated from Beaufort High School in 1941. The Honeycutt family had been part of Beaufort County since the early 1700's. As one might imagine, there were many Honeycutt families in the area. Maurice's branch of the Honeycutt family were patriots who had fought against the British in the Revolutionary War in battles all through South Carolina. As a result, these Honeycutts enjoyed the spoils of war and became politicians and owners of large tracts of land. Politics and land management were now the common trades of the Honeycutts.

Like most of the young men in Beaufort after December 7, 1941, Maurice joined the Marines and went to boot camp down the street at Parris Island. After serving as a hospital corpsman in World War II, he used the benefits from the G.I. Bill to go to school and to become a medical doctor. Maurice got his bachelor's degree in biology from the University of South Carolina. With some help from the local and state politicians who had known "Little Maurice" as a boy, he was able to graduate with a medical degree from the Medical University of South Carolina (MUSC) in Charleston in 1953 – the first doctor in his family. For the next three years, Dr. Honeycutt performed his residency at MUSC. Afterwards, he hired was hired as one of only a few doctors at the fledgling Beaufort Memorial that had only opened its doors twelve years earlier.

ooooo

It was a few weeks after the beginning of the New Year, 1980. Christine had almost completed the twenty-five miles from her house to Beaufort Memorial, when an ambulance passed her on the left. She was only one mile away. Already dressed in her candy striper uniform, she parked her Mt. Fuji blue, 1970 Datsun and looked toward the emergency entrance where the ambulance had pulled up. While walking toward the ambulance, two nurses pulled out the gurney. Christine heard urgent voices say that the gurney held thirty-one year old Jason McRae whose neck had been cut on the right side. The technician that rode in the back of the ambulance told the nurses that Jason had accidentally tripped, and landed onto a disc harrow stored in his barn. Christine knew that while the discs in a disc harrow were not extremely sharp because of their use in cultivating soil, they did have jagged edges that can blunt cut human flesh. Her father would regularly come in from the fields with cuts and abrasions from, what he called common farm accidents. At eighteen years old, Christine had seen her share of "common" farm accidents that took lives. At that moment, an emotion – not rage – not anger – more like empathy for Mr.

McRae took over. She could almost feel his fear and anger that this stupid accident might kill him.

Christine walked up to the gurney and asked, "What can I do?"

"Hold his hands to his side to keep him from lifting them up to the neck wound," said Nurse Lisa Hoffine. "The disc has cut much of the muscle on the right side. Fortunately, it has only nicked the carotid artery."

At fifty-eight years old, Lisa had seen her share of emergencies. She was only twenty-two when she became one of the first nurses at Beaufort Memorial in 1944. She was the most senior person at Beaufort Memorial. The Hoffines were another of the old families of Beaufort County. Many in her family had college degrees; mostly in law and banking. She was the first to go into the medical field.

Lisa was applying pressure to the wound so that the nick on the artery would not get bigger.

"Jason," she said, "you are at the hospital now. I have your cut covered with a bandage and my hand. You are going to be okay. Your family is right behind you, and will be here in a few minutes."

Renee Scott was the other nurse in the emergency room. She was a smart, pretty, African-American woman who had received her nursing degree in 1978 at the age of twenty-three. She was hired at Beaufort Memorial the same year. After the end of the Civil War, the Scott family had prospered from being mere share croppers to land owners who worked their own farms. Renee was the first in her family to receive a college degree. Like Christine Jesup, Renee had seen her share of farm accidents. She lost her brother to one when he fell off a tractor during the harvest. He crushed his skull on a rock. While her uncle drove the pickup truck as fast as he could, she sat in the bed of the truck, holding her brother's head in her lap. She held a towel to the wound, talking to him; telling him that they were on the way to the hospital. She felt his body go lifeless while traveling Highway 17. To this day, she remembered how helpless she felt, not knowing how to do more. She would learn how to do more.

"Renee!" urgently called Lisa, "Call Dr. Honeycutt. I think he is doing his rounds at the other end of the hospital."

"After you send the page, go get me some more bandages, Renee," said Lisa. Christine held both of Jason's hands in order to keep them by his side. Jason looked at Christine with fear in his eyes.

"Jason," said Christine, "it's me, Christine Jesup. You know me. I go to school with your younger sister, Marlene. When I was younger, I came to your daddy's house to spend the night on Halloween. You were still living at home then. You took me, Marlene, and those mean Sellers boys on a hayride. After the hay ride, the Sellers boys kept jumpin' out from behind trees and throwin' bugs on me and Marlene. We cried, and you run off those boys. I was only eight, and you took care of me then. Well, I am going to be here to help take care of you now. You don't worry none, you understand?"

Jason's eyes turned from fear to almost relief. While he was still scared, he knew he was with someone he trusted.

Dr. Honeycutt came through the swinging door into the ER. He was a tall man with the physique of a man much younger. The only sign of his actual age was his gray, "high and tight" Marine hair cut that he had first gotten 1941. He saw that Lisa was keeping pressure on Jason's neck wound. He saw Christine on the left side of the gurney, near the end, holding both of Jason's hands. He had seen Christine before, among the other candy stripers during Christmas and other holiday gatherings, but they had never spoken before.

"What's his name and what happened?" said Dr. Honeycutt to no one in particular.

Lisa said, "Jason McRae is a local farmer. While in his barn, he fell onto a disc harrow and cut the right side of his neck with a disc. Much of the bleeding is from a nick in his carotid. I am keeping pressure on the wound."

Dr. Honeycutt, thinking out loud, said, "These type discs are not very sharp, but are very jagged. The 'nick' in the artery is probably jagged, as well." For a moment, Christine forgot the situation, and was impressed that he would know what a disc harrow was.

"Lisa," said Dr. Honeycutt, "I need to see the wound to determine whether or not we have the capabilities here to fix this fellow."

"Jason?" he said, looking into his eyes, "I am Dr. Honeycutt. I need you to be very calm so I can look at what is going on here. Nurse Lisa and I will trade places. I will take a quick look at the wound. If we can, we will take care of you here. If things are more involved, you get a free ride to Charleston. Here we go." Dr. Honeycutt positioned himself to the right of Lisa. Just above a whisper, he said, "On the count of three: One, two, three!"

At that moment, Lisa removed her hand, and it was replaced with the left hand of Dr. Honeycutt. She immediately went to the surgery center to prepare, just in case.

With a smile, Dr. Honeycutt placed his other hand on Jason's chest. "That was step one. Let's see what is going on here."

Jason was calmer. Dr. Honeycutt eased the pressure on the wound. Slowly he lifted the bandage to reveal something that looked more like a gash than a cut. It was approximately three inches long, but not as deep. At its deepest point, the nick in the artery was visible. The only two people with Jason were Dr. Honeycutt and Christine Jesup – the candy striper.

The cold January air hit Jason's wound. Jason tensed up, causing his blood pressure to rise. The rise in blood pressure caused the nick in the artery to double in size with triple the amount of blood shooting out with every heartbeat. The squirting blood shot all over Dr. Honeycutt's white coat and onto the floor. The soiled bandage in his hand was not enough to stop this amount of blood.

He looked at Christine and said, "Girl, come here quickly! Take both of your hands and place them over the wound!"

Christine let go of Jason's hands and hurried to the side of the gurney, opposite Dr. Honeycutt.

"Like this," he said like a teacher, while taking Christine's hands and placing them over the wound.

With Dr. Honeycutt's hands over Christine's, he said, "You got it?"

"I got it," she said.

"Good." In a calm but concerned voice, Dr. Honeycutt said, "Now, I am going to let go. You will continue to keep pressure on his neck while I go find a cart with bandages and

things I can use. Do you understand?"

"Yes, sir," she said.

At about that time, Renee returned with the medical supplies she was sent to find. Dr. Honeycutt took several large bandages and went, once again, to the side of the gurney opposite Christine. He noticed that some of the blood that squirted on him had splashed on this young candy striper. Some of it was even in her hair.

He looked at Christine and said, "Very good job, young lady. Now," he said, looking down at the wound, "I want you to remove one hand at a time. I will place these bandages where your hands were. Nurse Renee will take over and apply pressure. Ready, set, go."

The bandages were placed on Jason's neck wound, and Renee took over applying pressure. A surgical assistant, who was standing nearby, grabbed the foot end of the gurney and rolled it toward the surgery center while Renee walked along, applying pressure.

While following Jason McRae to the surgical room, Dr. Honeycutt finally noticed the blood-soaked clothes on Christine.

"What is your name?"

"My name is Christine Jesup."

With a slight, Cheshire cat grin, he said, "Well, I think you helped save your first life today. Are you ready for another?"

This was the first time Christine had had a chance to think about anything. All of her actions, all of the commands she responded to, had been done without thinking. She looked down at the blood on her clothes, and at the ends of her brown hair. In front of her was the gore. In front of her was the smell of it all. It did not matter. These were the sights and smells of life saving. She liked it.

    With her own, slightly larger grin, she said to Dr. Honeycutt, "I think so."

Dr. Honeycutt had been a corpsman during the Battle of Iwo Jima. He had seen battle hardened Marines faint with only the half the blood spilled that day. Dr. Honeycutt thought to himself while heading to surgery, "This one. This one will save more lives."

2 - THE MAKING OF A BABY DOCTOR

After graduating at the top of her high school class in 1980, and receiving a full scholarship, Christine Jesup headed to the University of South Carolina in Columbia. She graduated with a degree in biology, which included other special courses she thought necessary for a medical degree. During her summer breaks, she continued her time at the Beaufort Memorial Hospital (Beaufort Memorial), this time as a paid nurse's assistant. When not working at Beaufort Memorial, she also helped around her family's farm back in Sheldon. Her summers were full.

Dr. Honeycutt was very influential in Christine's professional life. It was his letter of recommendation that got Christine into USC. He made sure that USC gave her every consideration. At the hospital, where she worked during the summer, he would talk with her about school and her experiences at college.

Like Dr. Honeycutt, Christine Jesup received her medical degree from MUSC. She graduated in the top one percent of her class in 1988. Also like Dr. Honeycutt, she did her residency at MUSC. Afterwards, she was hired as the first female doctor at Beaufort Memorial. Her first full year as a doctor was a great experience. Like her mentor predicted, she saved many lives.

ooooo

"Keep breathing, and push for me one more time, Sally," said Dr. Christine Jesup to Sally Flournoy.

Duke and Sally Flournoy were the proud parents of three, about to be four, children. The first three were boys. This baby, to Sally's delight, was a girl. Christine had both hands on the baby's head, doing her best to coax the baby out, at the same time knowing they come "when they darn well want to."

"The crown is out!" Christine said.

Duke was standing behind the delivery table, at the right side of Sally's head.

"Duke?" said Christine while not looking up, "Hold Sally's hands like we taught you and help her breathe. Tell her you love her. But don't let go of her hands. She just might smack you 'up side your head,'" she said, the local way, and taking a quick look up and winking.

"Here she comes!" Christine said to the room. With both hands on the head, she lifted up her left knee and put it against the delivery table.

She said to herself, "The head is right. The shoulders are right. The umbilical cord is right. All looks good."

"Here we go. Sally, really push this time," said Christine.

While pulling a little bit more, Christine said to Sally, "push...push...push...don't forget to breathe...push...she is here!"

Christine took the baby toward herself for a quick look. When she was satisfied, she handed the baby over to the nurse. After a few minutes, the baby, wrapped tightly in a pink cotton blanket, was laid in Sally's arms.

"What are you naming the baby?" asked Christine.

"We are naming her Naomi Isadora Flournoy, after my grandmothers. All my boys have names from Duke's family. "It's my turn," she said while looking down at the baby.

"Those are good, strong names," said Christine. "Congratulations."

3 - THE CONTRACTOR AND HIS ATTORNEY

"Why are you even bothering with a Notice to Bidders from the South Carolina Department of Transportation (SCDOT)?" said Byron Heard to Nathan Bishop over breakfast at Skip's Restaurant.

Nathan Bishop was the owner of Bishop Construction. He had taken over the roadway construction business after his father, Mit Bishop, passed away ten years ago. Nathan ate too much and drank too much. He partook too much of the traditional fried foods and sugary desserts of the South without an appropriate amount of exercise. His almost 300 pound profile was proof of that. His particular weakness was the daily breakfast meal at Skip's that usually included three fried eggs (over easy), fried potatoes, country ham (never city ham), a bowl of grits, and a separate plate of biscuits and gravy. To his credit, he would have sliced tomatoes when in season.

Byron Heard was a partner at the law firm of Heard, Dixon and Galloway. He was the oldest partner at the second-oldest law firm in Columbia. Always wearing a two-piece suit with ties far too wide for current fashion, he was known for his work in saving corporations millions in federal and state taxes. He was even better known for his corporate defense work. He was on the short list of all the major insurance companies in South Carolina. He was also on the "extra" short list of most of the major highway construction firms in the state. He had gotten to know Nathan Bishop when the federal government filed a Sherman Antitrust lawsuit against him and his buddies. Along with two other highway construction firms, Nathan had been very active in the act of collusion – bid rigging. Nathan, along with the others, would get together every time a Notice to Bidders was published by the SCDOT that involved Beaufort County. Each would take a turn being the "lowest bidder," to assure each got a turn being the bid winner.

"Why do I bother?" he said, "Because I am sick and damn tired of fillin' pot holes, fixin' driveways, and pavin' every cow trail in Beaufort County, that's why!"

After his conviction for violating the Sherman Antitrust Act, Bishop Construction was forbidden to bid on SCDOT projects for five years, in addition to a $10,000 fine.

"We had a good thing goin', Byron. If Mike Babbage could have only kept it in his pants, we'd still be goin' strong."

Many in the South Carolina highway construction business wondered how Nathan Bishop and his co-conspirators got off so lightly. Normally, a person convicted of violating the Sherman Antitrust Act was forbidden from ever bidding on another road construction project, and given a hefty fine, plus jail time. Nathan had many relationships in the SCDOT. Many of these relationships were with people in upper management whose pasts were as pure as lard. Knowing where the skeletons were buried enabled him and his buddies to leverage a lighter settlement.

Mike Babbage, one of Nathan's co-conspirators, and also a married man for twenty years, had decided to move up his status to "Sugar Daddy" and have a girlfriend on the side, complete with an apartment for his younger honey and a monthly stipend to cover her expenses. Mike kept all of his "off the record" business documents at this apartment so that others at his company would not know about his arrangement with Nathan Bishop and Jerry Strickland. It all came apart when Mike's wife, Julie, found out about the girlfriend and the apartment. If a man is not going to do his own laundry, he'd better make sure he takes out the jewelry and hotel receipts from his own pockets. Julie was smart. Instead of immediately confronting Mike with the affair, she planned things out. While the girlfriend was gone, Julie broke into her apartment. A credit card and butter knife were all that was needed. No marks were left. Neatly stacked in the second bedroom were business boxes. Having helped Mike start his highway construction company fifteen years before, she knew what construction plans, specifications, and bid documents looked like. She also found a legal pad that contained columns for Nathan Bishop, Jerry Strickland, and Mike Babbage. The rows contained the names of the different highway projects put out by the SCDOT in the last ten years, along with each company's bid. She noticed that her husband's company was winning every third highway project. "Oh my God!" thought Julie. "I guess he really is that stupid." At the same time the divorce papers were being delivered to Mike Babbage, a copy of the legal pad, along with other incriminating notes and documents, were being delivered to the Beaufort County District Attorney.

ooooo

Nathan's daddy, Mit Bishop, started Bishop Construction in 1947. As a Seabee during WWII, he had learned how to use heavy equipment to build roads, bridges and air fields; usually under enemy fire. He learned how to coordinate men and machines to get the job done. Years later, after starting his roadway construction company and while working with his heavy equipment, he thought it odd that, from time to time, he would still look down to make sure his rifle was close by.

Mit and Barbara Bishop had four children. Nathan was the oldest. He started working for his dad at ten years old. Nathan learned all there was to know about the highway building business. He worked the spreaders, the dump trucks, the pavers – all the machinery. When a Notice to Bidders would come in from the SCDOT, he worked next to Mit to develop the bid for the job. Nathan knew the road building business. Unfortunately, he learned it when there was little competition, and the federal dollars were plentiful.

Mit Bishop died of lung cancer. All of those years of breathing road dust and liquid asphalt fumes finally took its toll. As expected, Nathan became the new owner of Bishop Construction. He worked hard to keep the company going. However, when things got difficult, he decided to take a less honorable route. It was unfortunate that honesty and integrity were not an inherited trait.

"Byron," said Nathan, looking straight at him over his biscuits and gravy, "I'm going to get this road construction contract come hell or high water. I've been working these piddly jobs for ten years now just to keep a little cash flow."

"What is your strategy this time?" said Byron, with a slight smirk.

"My 'ultimate' strategy," said Nathan, "is to get back into the good graces of the SCDOT. To do that, I need to make sure I am the lowest bidder, no matter who else is bidding. I've managed to save up a little cash. I will need that money when my bid will actually cost me money."

"How is that smart, Nathan?" said Byron. "You have to make money or you could bankrupt."

"I will be okay on this one," said Nathan. "I just need this one."

4 - THE BIDDING

This particular roadway construction project was very straightforward – a simple two inch overlay of bituminous asphalt pavement over an 8.1 mile section of State Road S-7-3, otherwise locally known as Old Sheldon Church Road which ran to the Sheldon Church ruins nearby. Sheldon Church was originally constructed in the mid 1700's. Burned by the British in 1789, it was rebuilt and burned again, this time by General Sherman near the end of the Civil War. This was a two-lane rural road lined with many old homes on large tracts of land. The Spanish moss-covered oaks and other trees were very close to the edge of the road. Time and wear had taken its toll on this section. Heavy logging trucks, dump trucks, and other heavy vehicles had created dangerous pot holes and depressions in the travel lanes. In addition, vehicles that inadvertently left the asphalt road and drove on the earthen shoulder had depressed the soil next to the roadway edge. This caused a significant shoulder drop-off that made it very difficult for a driver to re-enter the travel lane.

Included in the roadway contract was the customary language that required the winning bidder to abide by all of the requirements depicted in the scope of work outlined in the SCDOT drawings, and all the requirements written in the SCDOT Standard Specifications for Highway Construction – 1986 Edition – otherwise known as the "Red Book" – to those in the South Carolina road building industry.

While not large compared to past roadway projects, this was one of the largest projects in several years – so large in fact, the SCDOT decided to help the competitive process by continuing an old custom. All of the bidders were brought in and put up in a hotel the night before the bid opening – the same hotel, paid for by the SCDOT. The logic behind this was that it would allow the smaller companies an equal advantage in the bidding process by just being present. What it actually did was to allow the closer and larger company owners access to everyone's bids. No one would knowingly give out his bid. But, after a few rum and Cokes, the numbers "accidently" fell out of their mouths.

Two of the most significant costs on any roadway project using bituminous asphalt concrete (asphalt) are the asphalt being laid down; and the signage, cones, and man power to advise and protect the public during a roadway project. The asphalt is composed of bitumen (a tar-like substance), and aggregate (gravel and sand). Depending on whether one is placing the bottom layer of a new road, or placing the top layer to drive on, the types and amounts of bitumen and aggregate are different. If the ingredients are not of high quality, and are not proportioned properly, the asphalt is ruined. Problems from an improper asphalt mix range from rutting, bitumen bleeding from the surface, to instability, meaning it cannot hold its shape when loaded. Closing the roadway is rarely an option for an existing road. When paving one lane, the other lane must remain open; which requires barrels, cones, "Follow Me" trucks to guide the traffic through the work zone, and the necessary personnel.

For this roadway project, Nathan decided that the only way to win (besides getting the other bidders drunk the night before the bid opening) was to reduce his cost to the bare bones for the asphalt and construction zone safety. For the asphalt, the SCDOT provides ranges for each component of the asphalt mix. With a lower bitumen content, and an aggregate that does not take too much work to break up, the cost per ton of asphalt will be lower. For work zone safety, Nathan decided to rent the cones, barrels, and other work zone and traffic safety devices. The plan was to only use the devices at locations where work was actually being performed. Besides, why would they be needed when nothing was going on?

As designed, Bishop Construction Company won the bid to resurface Old Sheldon Church Road. After winning a bid, and before the "Notice to Proceed" was given by the SCDOT to start work, a preconstruction meeting was held just before Christmas to discuss the particulars of the upcoming roadway project. The preconstruction meeting was held at the SCDOT district office in North Charleston. Presiding over the meeting was Drew Richards, Professional Engineer (PE). He received his bachelor's degree in civil engineering from the Citadel in 1965. He immediately went to the work for the SCDOT as an assistant field engineer in the North Charleston office. After the required four years of working under a licensed professional engineer, he took the PE test, and passed. He became the assistant district engineer in the North Charleston office. Drew had every intention of moving up by working as an engineer, project manager, and higher, in the SCDOT headquarters in Columbia. Civil engineering graduates from the Citadel expected, and normally got, preferential treatment when working for the SCDOT. Unfortunately for Drew, work habits, politics, and other obstacles got in the way. Now, after twenty-seven years with the SCDOT, he was bored doing the same work, in the same rural areas, for the same people year after year. Over time, the attention he used to give to his work had suffered. One of Drew's duties (which, in the past had been his most favorite) was riding over all of the back roads in all of the six counties in the district he worked in. The purpose of this was to see if there was anything wrong with the roads that needed attention. Drew used to find pot-holes, vegetation too close to the roadway, missing or broken signage, and shoulder problems which he would eagerly report to those in Columbia. These days, he did not notice as much, and was not too eager to alert his superiors if he did.

"Nathan," said Drew, "it is good to see you again. It has been too many years since we last spoke."

Drew, while not particularly hard working, was honest. He loathed Nathan and his cronies for what they had done, and wanted to get this meeting over as soon as possible. His resentment for having to work with Nathan was very apparent.

While reading a memo not related to the meeting, he said to Nathan, "You understand that from the date this office issues you the "Notice to Proceed", to the date this office issues you the "Letter of Acceptance" that you have complete responsibility of the section of Old Sheldon Church Road outlined in the construction documents."

"Yes, I understand perfectly," said Nathan thinking how unnecessary this meeting was.

"Because of the size of this project, normal Quality Control and Quality Assurance protocols will be followed," said Drew.

Normal Quality Control and Quality Assurance protocols dictated that the contractor would perform the tests on the asphalt mixture at a lab they hired, and provide the results to the SCDOT. This was the quality control part. The quality assurance part would be the SCDOT field personnel taking their own asphalt for testing in the SCDOT labs.

"Again, I understand perfectly," said Nathan becoming a little agitated.

Drew looked up from his memo and said, "It is important that you follow the SCDOT testing procedures. To not follow them would mean a reduction in the amount we pay you."

"I have a question," said Nathan.

"Yes?" said Drew

"Just so we are clear. All that you and the others here in this office are looking for me to only complete is the scope of work outlined in these construction drawings and specifications, correct?" said Nathan.

Drew thought to himself, "What is he trying to get away with? This is a very simple project."

Then he said to Nathan, "The plans and specifications outline the scope of work plainly. As long as you properly overlay the road, and abide by the provisions in the Red Book, I believe we will get along fine."

Nathan said, "That is all I want to know."

5 - ROAD CONSTRUCTION

For the past seven years, Trevor Arnold had worked for Bishop Construction Company. During his first two years, he had worked himself up from "gopher" (gopher coffee, gopher lunch, gopher this and that) to someone Nathan Bishop trusted to lead the larger jobs. Then, Nathan's Sherman Antitrust conviction stopped his advancement cold. Rather than quit the company, Trevor decided to stick it out. Besides, as a high school dropout and with a juvenile record not as clean as it could be, his prospects were not encouraging. Nathan kept Trevor employed, if only to have someone that reminded him of better days. Trevor was the crew chief who fixed the pot-holes, driveways and all of the other minor jobs Nathan could get from the powers that be in Beaufort County. While Nathan never told Trevor about the relationships or the details involving the collusion (or anything else for that matter), he knew that Trevor could be counted on to show up to work, and to do what he was told.

It was the first Monday morning after Christmas. Trevor was waiting outside the offices for Nathan to arrive at the Yard, the home of Bishop Construction Company, that had been developed by Nathan's daddy many years ago. In its heyday, the Yard's two large steel buildings contained a large heavy equipment maintenance area, a dry area for the storage of aggregate and bitumen when small batches were necessary, and an area for the storage of safety barrels, cones, signs, and other devices used to warn the driving public during a road construction project. Because of the recent misfortunes, most of the equipment had been sold to keep the company afloat. All that was left to be stored in the metal buildings was an asphalt spreader, a dump truck, a few pickup trucks, and some antiquated asphalt testing equipment. The offices were sparse as well. Before the downsizing, there had been an administrative staff of ten to handle all the day-to-day operations. Now it was Nathan, Trevor, and Sally Crews. Sally answered the telephone, was Nathan's secretary, took care of all the federal, state and local taxes, handled payroll, and all other administrative tasks.

Nathan pulled up next to Trevor, who was leaning against his parked truck. He stepped out and said, "You ready to go to work?"

"I was born ready," said Trevor.

"To celebrate this occasion, I am promoting you to project manager."

"Thanks. Who did I beat out for the job?" said Trevor, with a slight grin.

"Don't be a smart ass," said Nathan, pointing his index finger toward him.

"We are going to need a crew, and in a hurry, don't you think?" said Trevor.

"Yeah, but we have that covered," said Nathan. "We are going to use the same people we have been using for the past five years for the pot holes and driveways. I work them like subcontractors. I can't afford real employees at the moment. Besides, less paperwork," he said with a smile.

"It's kind of cold right now. The Red Book says that we cannot pave until March 1st," said Trevor.

"That book is for the entire state of South Carolina. That spec is more for the mountains in the Up Country. Besides, we are in the Low Country. I think we can get Drew Richards' permission to start earlier," said Nathan.

"What about the asphalt testing requirement? The contract states that we are to take samples every 1000 feet of pavement lane. Our testing equipment isn't exactly working at the moment," said Trevor.

"Damn, that boy asks a lot of questions," thought Nathan to himself. "He's eager if nothing else."

Nathan said, "One of your first jobs is to get that testing equipment working again," he said. "The contract states that we are to provide a field laboratory. It doesn't say it has to be clean and pretty. Once the trailer is set up with electricity and water, put the testing equipment in and see what you can do. All we have to do is satisfy the SCDOT. After that, who cares?"

Nathan turned towards the office, and said to Trevor, "Sally and I have a lot of work to do. We have to submit a performance bond and proof of general liability insurance." Nathan stops at the door, and turns around toward Trevor. "You and I need to talk about the asphalt job mix formula we need to get to our esteemed engineer Richards. Once approved, we may have to make a few changes in the field."

"What about testing?" said Trevor. "It may get noticed."

"Careful selection, my man. We just need to be careful where we take our samples," said Nathan.

ooooo

With the written permission of Drew Richards, PE, of the SCDOT, the asphalt overlay project of Old Sheldon Church Road began on February 17, 1992. The paving started at the northern end of the project. Overlay projects for two-lane roads are accomplished by paving one lane at a time, utilizing a rolling construction zone. Before the paving may begin, all the warning signs, barrels, and cones must be in place so that a lane can be closed for paving. Signs should be placed well in advance of the construction activity to warn drivers that there will be a lane closure. Barrels and cones are placed to divert the drivers to the open lane, and to keep them off the new paving. As the work progresses, the signs and barrels are moved to where the work is actually taking place. After the hot asphalt is placed, it is compacted to its proper density using a compaction roller. When the asphalt has cooled to the satisfaction of the SCDOT inspectors on site, the lane is reopened, and the barrels, cones and signs are moved to the new work location.

Trevor Arnold was a very busy man. Not only was he the project manager directing the paving operations, he was in charge of obtaining all of the safety equipment, taking and testing the asphalt cores, and making sure the safety equipment was moved to the proper location for the next day's operations. With so much to do, he was only able to pave about one mile a day. This was bad, given that he had to rent all of the signs, the barrels and cones, and the compaction roller; and to work with a crew that, up until about two weeks ago, had known only pot holes and driveways. Nathan, for his part, was working with Sally every day, making sure that all of the paperwork that these types of projects create was completed and on time. When time permitted, he drove through the project on his way to see Drew Richards. Nathan wanted to make sure he was in front of any problem that might come up. After about two work weeks, which included two days of setting up, the 12 feet wide by 8.1 mile southbound lane would soon be completed.

It was a late Thursday afternoon. All paving operations had been completed for the day. Like the end of every work day, Trevor drove to the Yard. He walked into Nathan's office and found him looking at spreadsheets. The concerned look on Nathan's face was not good.

"What-cha' looking at?" said Trevor.

Nathan looked up from the spreadsheets. "A money pit, that's what. Asphalt has really gone up in the past few years. More than I thought. How's it going with the paving?"

"Fine," said Trevor. "We are going to finish the southbound lane tomorrow. Mr. Bishop," said Trevor with wide eyes and a smile, "it feels good to work again."

Nathan did not give much thought to Trevor's enthusiasm. In fact, he thought it somewhat childish. Besides, there was money to be made. Or more accurately, there was money to be saved.

"Have you been keeping up with your expenses on this job?" said Nathan.

"As best I can, Mr. Bishop," said Trevor, noting that Nathan did not want to share in the tender moment.

"So have I," said Nathan with a lower, directed voice. "There are going to be some changes."

"What do you mean?" said Trevor.

After a few moments of thought, Nathan asked Trevor, "How many safety barrels are we renting at the moment?"

"Five hundred."

"And where are they being used?"

"Well, where the paving work is going on, you know, to close the lane so we can pave it," said Trevor.

"You can't need all of them there. Where else?" said Nathan.

"I found several places, several shoulders, where the drop-off was four, sometimes six inches, before we ever got there. After we finished pavin', I've been placing the barrels along the shoulder edge to warn folks; warn them not to drive off the road."

"Did anyone with the SCDOT tell you to do that?"

"No. It just seemed the right thing to do," said Trevor.

Life is not really about big choices. Sure, who we marry, joining the military, and where we live are all important. But it is the small choices that direct our lives. Do I watch TV or finish my homework? Do I buy two packs of cigarettes a day, or save that money to buy a car? Do I remove the safety barrels from the shoulder, or do I leave them to warn drivers – and risk alerting the SCDOT to a shoulder problem that they are going to make Bishop Construction Company fix?

"Trevor," said Nathan, "have you spoken to anyone about the shoulders?"

"No, sir."

"Good. I believe we are safe to assume that the SCDOT already knows about the shoulders. They've owned the road for decades. How could they not know? Besides, if they thought it was a problem, they would have made it part of this contract. Drew Richards never said a thing to me."

Nathan looked firmly at Trevor and said, "Drew Richards does not like me, and is not shy about it. If he thought he could force me to bring up those shoulders at my expense, he'd put the screws to me in a minute. This is what I want you to do. Each one of those barrels is costing me one dollar a day. That is five hundred dollars a day for stupid barrels! I want you to first gather up all those barrels you placed at the shoulders. Do this tomorrow. Then, I want you to return 250 barrels to the rental shop in town before they close. Use the remaining barrels only at the paving work area. Do you understand me?"

"Yes sir," said Trevor. "We still have the northbound lane to do. What about those shoulder drop-offs?"

Nathan stood up slowly and said, "Trevor, I'm not sure you do understand. If you put those barrels against the shoulders, Drew Richards will come beboppin' by and see those barrels. He will say to himself, (Nathan brought in his chin and talked like a professor) 'Well, what do we have here? We have a dangerous shoulder drop-off. Since my good friend Nathan Bishop has contractual ownership of this piece of earth, he will have to bring up this section of shoulder, and ALL the other sections of shoulders I am about to find. It is the least he could do.' If he finds this, and makes an issue out of it, I will not be able to finish the project. The performance bond will kick in. Because I will never get insurance again, I am out of the road construction business. Is that plain enough for you?"

"Yes, Mr. Bishop," said Trevor. "We will be starting the northbound lane on Monday morning. The barrels will only be there."

Nathan sat back down and looked at the spreadsheet again. It took a second, but Trevor finally got the hint that he was dismissed.

As he left Nathan's office, Trevor thought to himself, "He sure says 'I' a lot."

6 - THE INCIDENT

Thirteen year old Margaret "Maggie" Louise Bunn was a patient of Dr. Christine Jesup. In addition to providing pediatric care, Christine was also, unfortunately, Maggie's obstetrician. Soon after Maggie's thirteenth birthday, Maggie got pregnant. The father of the baby was not known to anyone but Maggie. Maggie believed that she was in love, and that he loved her. Even in her bliss, she knew what her daddy would do if he knew the father's name. The sheriff's office was involved as well. They had their suspicions; but were not sharing them with Maggie's daddy. They also knew what her daddy would do. Honor killings were not unusual in the Low Country, even in 1992. Be that as it may, Maggie was Christine's patient. Christine knew that Maggie's pregnancy might be difficult because she was so young. Maggie's mother would bring her to in to Beaufort Memorial once a month for a checkup. Christine was concerned that after eight months, the baby had not turned head down.

On the morning of Monday, March 1, Maggie woke up not feeling well. She scooted herself up with her arms to sit up in the bed. Her legs felt wet. She looked down at her groin area and saw deep red, fresh blood on her nightgown and on the bed sheets. A cold fear gripped her. For a second she did not know what to do. She then screamed, "Mama, Mama! Oh my God, Mama!" Maggie's continued screams could be heard throughout the house.

Maggie's mother came running from the main level, up the stairs, and into Maggie's room. At first, she looked at Maggie's crying, terrified face. She then looked down at the bloody bed. "Oh, Lord," she thought to herself. She ran to Maggie and tried to calm her down by hugging her head.

She said in a calm voice, "Maggie, I'm going downstairs and call Dr. Jesup. I will be back in a minute. Now these things happen all the time. Your baby - my grandbaby is fine. You are fine. I'll be right back."

"Mama, I'm sorry what I done. I didn't know I'd be trouble to you and daddy."

Looking straight into Maggie's eyes, her mother said "Baby girl, you need to stop thinking about that. You are about to be a mama, yourself. You need to be thinking about you and this baby. Nothing, and I mean nothing, else matters right now. You hear?"

"Yes, Mama" said Maggie. She felt reassured knowing that this woman, her mama, would crash the gates of hell to keep her and this baby safe.

ooooo

"This is Dr. Jesup," said Christine Jesup from the ER nurse's station.

"Dr. Jesup, this is Mrs. Bunn, Maggie's mama. Maggie's in trouble."

"What's wrong?"

"She woke up this morning bleeding from her privates. There is blood all over her and the bed. What do I do?"

"After we hang up, I will call the Yemassee Fire Department. You call them also and give them your address. I will tell them what you told me. I am on my way with an ambulance to get Maggie."

"Renee!" said Christine while walking to the ER door, toward two Emergency Medical Technicians (EMT) who were standing next to their ambulance, drinking coffee.

"Yes, doctor," said Renee Scott.

"Call the Yemassee Fire Department. Tell them that, if they have not already, the will be getting a call from the mother of Maggie Bunn. Tell them that Maggie is my thirteen year old patient and has been getting regular OB/GYN exams. She is almost nine months along and the baby has not turned. This morning she woke up and found she was bleeding vaginally. Tell them to stabilize Maggie, and to prepare her for transport to Beaufort for a Cesarean section."

"Yes ma'am," said Renee. "Do you want me to alert Dr. Honeycutt and get the operating room ready?"

"Yes," said Dr. Jesup. "And have four pints of B-positive blood ready."

While walking toward the two EMT's, Christine said, "We have a pregnant thirteen year old in Yemassee that might need a C-section. Let's go." Both EMT's, in one quick movement, threw their coffees onto the pavement, and their cups onto the floorboard of the ambulance.

The two EMT's were Beatrice "Betty" Pitts, and Gerald Toombs. Betty Pitts was fifty years old, with dyed dark brown hair, and was senior EMT at Beaufort Memorial. Starting in the late 1960's, she was the first female EMT to work for Beaufort Memorial. Gerald Toombs was a recent hire for Beaufort Memorial. Gerald had been a medical technician for the Army during the first Iraq war.

Christine opened the back door and climbed into the ambulance. From the outside, Gerald made sure the doors were closed. Betty and Gerald got into the front seat, with Betty driving.

Betty turned around and said to Dr. Jesup, "Where we going?"

"27 Maple Street, Yemassee." Christine had been there many times before.

Betty said, "Old Sheldon Church Road is the fastest way. They finished the southbound lane last week. The signs and barrels are up on this end. Once they let us through, it is a straight shot to Yemassee. Buckle up, Doctor."

"Right," said Dr. Jesup while looking away, thinking about Maggie.

The ride to Yemassee was uneventful; except for negotiating the construction zone at the south end of Old Sheldon Church Road. Once they had passed the construction zone, it was a 55-plus mph ride all the way. The whole time, while sitting in her seat, Christine thought of how Maggie and the baby, might be bleeding to death. The death of an elderly patient was sad, but not a tragedy. It was when babies die that it becomes hard to accept. Even though she was pregnant, Christine still thought of Maggie as a child. "To lose two babies at once?" thought Dr. Jesup. "No!"

The ambulance pulled up to Maggie's house. The Yemassee firemen were with Maggie in her room. They had her strapped onto a gurney and were about to bring her downstairs when the ambulance arrived. Christine went into the house and saw from that bottom of the stairs that Maggie was coming down.

Christine said, "Bring her down carefully, fellas. Let's get her on the road as quick as we can." She looked toward Lieutenant Mitch Bonner, at the head of the gurney, and asked, "How is the bleeding?"

"It appears to be a one-time vaginal discharge. No other blood was noted. I understand there are complications with the pregnancy?" said Mitch Bonner.

"Yes," said Christine. "The baby has not turned."

"We'll get her in the ambulance," said Lieutenant Bonner as he reached the bottom of the stairs. He looked down at Maggie and said, smiling, "You be strong, girl. You're going to be a mama today."

Maggie's eyes were shut as she was being carried down the stairs. Her lips were moving while she quietly said the Lord's Prayer. After Lieutenant Bonner spoke to her, she opened her eyes as if she had found the answer to her prayer.

Behind the firemen was Maggie's mother. She said, "I just called Maggie's daddy. He is on his way here to get me. We will follow right behind you."

"Y'all don't take too long. Y'all don't want to miss the birth," said Dr. Jesup in a reassuring voice.

Maggie was loaded up into the ambulance. Her gurney was mechanically fastened to the floor of the ambulance. She was strapped into the gurney. Next to Maggie was Christine, in the jump seat next to the patient's head. It was specifically designed for doctors to sit in while a patient was being transported. Betty and Gerald were in the front, with Betty driving. For the first couple of miles, there were no problems. Christine held Maggie's hand while talking about anything except the baby.

"Doctor Christine. My belly feels funny," said Maggie

"What do you mean by funny, Maggie?" said Dr. Jesup.

Maggie's eyes went wide open and then she screamed, "It hurts! It hurts! My belly hurts!"

A second discharge of blood soaked the white sheet covering Maggie. Christine unbelted herself from her seat and moved to examine Maggie and the baby.

Trying not to scare her, Dr. Jesup said, "Let's see how you two are doing." Dr. Jesup unbuckled herself from the jump seat.

Betty and Gerald had heard their fair share of screaming before. In fact, they were somewhat expecting it. It did not startle Betty. Before the screaming occurred, she had been thinking to herself how smooth Old Sheldon Church Road was. This new pavement was a nice ride.

Just as they were starting the left curve past the intersection at Cotton Hall Road, a deer jumped from the left side of the road. Betty saw the open shoulder to her right and turned the wheel toward it. At fifty-plus miles per hour, and with a wide shoulder with no obstructions, this seemed like the right thing to do. Rather than a normal transition onto a shoulder (as she had done many times before to miss a deer), the right side of the ambulance felt like it went down a large drop onto the shoulder. The ambulance swayed from the sudden vertical drop of the right side. Betty yelled, "Jesus H. Christ, what was that?" The deer, startled by the ambulance, turned back towards the woods. With only the right side of the ambulance on the shoulder, Betty began to turn the steering wheel to left to remount the road. She kept turning to the left, but the ambulance stayed on the shoulder. She turned more to the left, but the pavement kept crumbling underneath the right front tire. Finally, the tire grabbed the pavement, and the ambulance lunged upward and onto the roadway. Because the front wheels were turned so far to the left, the ambulance steered directly into the other lane. Betty saw a pickup truck coming directly at the ambulance. She yelled, "Oh God!!!" and instinctively turned hard and fast to the right to miss the pickup coming at her. The top-heavy ambulance then rolled onto its side. The ambulance was sliding, top first, towards a large oak tree. Everyone in the ambulance was screaming to God, their mothers, and to their loved ones, as the ambulance hurled toward the tree – then it crashed. The tree smashed into the ambulance top at the wall between the cab and the patient area, almost cutting the ambulance in two. Everyone was knocked unconscious – except for Maggie.

The first thing Christine sensed when she awoke was the smell of dirt under her face. Then she heard people talking. She thought she heard them talking to Maggie. "You be still now. We are getting y'all to the hospital directly," she heard someone say. As she opened her eyes, she saw flashing blue and red lights. People were running in every direction. She saw gurneys being lifted into other ambulances. Christine realized that she was on the ground outside the ambulance. "I've got to help," she thought to herself. She realized that she could not move her arms or legs.

"Christine, Christine, I'm Lieutenant Bonner. You remember me from Maggie's house? You have an injury at the back of your head. Me and my boys are going to turn you over and get you stabilized. We are taking you directly to Charleston Medical."

Christine was lifted into an ambulance and began her trip to Charleston. Her eyes were open. She heard the EMT talking to her. But the only thought running over and over through her mind was "I cannot move!"

ooooo

As promised, Christine went directly to Charleston Medical, where she was immediately taken to surgery to evaluate the damage to her spine. Maggie was taken to Beaufort Memorial where she eventually had her baby boy. She lost a lot of blood, but was able to deliver successfully with the help of Dr. Honeycutt. Betty Pitts broke her hip. After her surgery, she began a long recovery period requiring weekly physical therapy sessions. Gerald Toombs broke his right forearm, not from the immediate impact of the tree, but from using his right arm to break the door and windshield glass to free himself after the tree impact. Even with a broken arm, Gerald had been able to tell the truck driver that was almost hit to go to a neighboring house to call for help.

ooooo

From nothingness, Christine regained consciousness. She realized she was lying in a hospital bed. From the mask over her nose and mouth, oxygen was being pumped into her to wake her from the anesthesia. She opened her eyes and saw her daddy on her right side, and Dr. Honeycutt on her left; each holding her hand. She looked into her daddy's eyes and saw that he has been crying. She tried to turn her head toward Dr. Honeycutt, but

29

realized she was wearing a cervical collar to immobilize her head. "Why am I wearing this?" she thought to herself. She moved her gaze toward Dr. Honeycutt.

"Christine, you're at Charleston Medical," said Dr. Honeycutt. With a forced smile, he added, "Maggie and the baby are doing fine. She had a C-section as you suggested. Betty Pitts broke her hip, had a surgery, and is now in recovery. Gerald Toombs broke his arm. He will be fine." In one blink, his lips went tight and horizontal. She had seen that look on his face before. It was the look he got before delivering bad news. "You've been in surgery for the past six hours. I'll be plain with you. You have a spinal cord injury between vertebrae C4 and C5. The swelling makes it difficult to determine the extent of the injury." Dr. Honeycutt went on about what the other doctors thought, and about what would be done next. Christine stared up toward the ceiling and fixed her gaze on decorative holes in the tile ceiling. "Spinal cord injury," she said to herself. She then looked down toward her hands. She couldn't feel her daddy's touch. She looked down toward her feet. She couldn't make them move. She looked at Dr. Honeycutt, and yelled in her mind, "Quadriplegic!"

Dr. Honeycutt stayed with Christine for two days after the incident. At that time, the news was not good – probable permanent spinal cord damage between the C4 and C5 vertebrae.

7 - THE INVESTIGATION

It was the third day after the incident, a late Thursday afternoon, and Dr. Honeycutt was sitting at his desk with a glass of bourbon and a document entitled, "Incident Report," prepared by South Carolina State Trooper Steven McPherson in the Beaufort headquarters. Dr. Honeycutt had cashed in a few favors and had it faxed directly to his office as soon as it was ready. Leaning forward over the desk, he read the findings of the investigating trooper as to the cause of the crash. The report showed the date and time of the crash, the clear and dry weather at the time of the crash, and had a paragraph about how a witness saw Betty Pitts attempt to miss a deer, and how she went onto the shoulder and tried to get back onto the road. Under the section entitled, "Contributing Factors," the trooper had written "deep shoulder drop-off." "What could that mean?" thought Dr. Honeycutt. He leaned back into his leather chair, still holding the report with both hands. He looked toward his telephone, and thought to himself, "I need to call Cephas."

Cephas Hampton was Dr. Honeycutt's first cousin on his mother's side. Because there were too many family members named "Peter" (which means "Rock" in Greek), the name Cephas ("Rock" in Aramaic) was given to him. Even though Cephas was five years younger than Dr. Honeycutt, they had been fairly close from the time Cephas was ten and Dr. Honeycutt was fifteen. There were other lawyers in the family, but Cephas really impressed Dr. Honeycutt because he had become a partner in one of the largest law firms in Columbia: Deal, Gossick & Hampton.

"Cephas, this is Maurice."

"Maurice!," said Cephas. "How are you doing down there in the Low Country?"

"We're fine here. How's your mama?" said Dr. Honeycutt.

"She's fine. She misses your mama terrible. When I see her, all she talks about is her sister, and how they will be together in Glory soon," said Cephas.

"Soon enough, I'm sure."

"Soon enough. What's going on?" said Cephas, hearing the

melancholy tone in his cousin's voice.

"I've got a young doctor that may need your help," said Dr. Honeycutt.

Dr. Honeycutt went on to tell Cephas what had happened to Dr. Jesup. It was his medical opinion that her injuries were severe, and that, barring some miracle, she would be a quadriplegic for life. For many years, Dr. Jesup would require twenty-four hour care. He told Cephas about the trooper's report, and that it said that a contributing factor was "deep shoulder drop-off."

"What does that mean, Cephas?"

"I'm not sure, Maurice, but I have a man that can find out for us. His name is William Buttermore. He is a former state trooper. He now works for me as an investigator. Fax me what you have; tonight if you can. Bill and I will go over it in the morning. Do Christine and her family know I'm looking at this?" said Cephas.

"Not yet," said Maurice. "I'm going to see her in Charleston this weekend. I'll talk to them then. It's just her and her daddy."

"I see," said Cephas. "Please tell them that I will probably send Bill to the incident site to see if there is anything there. If there's something to talk about, I will call you afterwards to set something up where all of us can meet. Sound good?"

"Sounds good," said Dr. Honeycutt. "Thank you, Cephas."

"No problem. Y'all be good."

"Y'all be good," said Dr. Honeycutt as he hung up the telephone.

ooooo

The next morning, Cephas was sitting at his desk when he heard William "Bill" Buttermore in the reception area. Even though Bill was a full time employee, he did not have an office. He did not need one. His work kept him on the road all the time. With a degree in criminal justice, and as a retired South Carolina state trooper with twenty years of service, he had developed a very useful skill set. He was adept at courthouse research, witness interviews, and discovering other facts mere mortals never could. Unfortunately, his love of the job, and his love of the road, did not mix well with matrimonial pursuits. He was twice divorced. Cephas had helped him with both.

Bill Buttermore could talk to anyone about anything. He had an uncanny ability to sell himself as a trusted listener. His state trooper friends would jokingly say that that Bill could sell ice at the North Pole. When not overly busy, Bill liked to use his conversational skills to chat up Cyndi Carday, the recently-single front deck receptionist. Bill, leaning on the reception deck, was in a deep conversation with Cyndi about upcoming local events when he heard from down the hall, "Oh brother Billy, leave Cyndi alone and come talk with me for a minute. I've got something for you to do." Bill leaned back from the desk, flashed a smile at Cyndi, and said, "I'll talk with you later." As Bill walked down the hall toward Cephas' office, Cyndi smiled and thought to herself, "That man is a rascal."

"What-cha' got, bossman?" said Bill.

"Did you hear about that ambulance that crashed in Beaufort County on Monday?" said Cephas.

"I did," said Bill. "I heard it was pretty bad. Did anyone die?"

"Worse," said Cephas. "There was a doctor named Christine Jesup, in the back helping a pregnant thirteen year old. Christine was not strapped in when the accident occurred. My cousin, Maurice Honeycutt, called me last night and told me that she is a quadriplegic. The girl and her baby are fine. They were strapped in tight. One EMT broke her hip. The other broke his arm."

"Damn," said Bill. "I assume the doctor works with your cousin?"

"That's right," said Cephas. "He sent me a copy of the trooper's report last night. What he called about was the 'Contributing Factors' section that said, 'deep shoulder drop-off.' Have you ever dealt with that before?"

"Many times," said Bill. "A low shoulder drop-off makes it hard for a vehicle to re-enter the road."

"Interesting," said Cephas. "Where did you learn that?"

"I went to a roadway safety seminar in Atlanta before I came to work for you. One of the speakers spoke about the dangers of shoulder drop-offs," said Bill.

Cephas said, "While everything is fresh, go down there first thing this morning and find out what you can. I'm not sure there is a case, but I want to do Maurice this favor. Come see me early Monday."

"Will do," said Bill. He turned and walked toward the front door. Walking by Cyndi, he said, "Got to go to work, darlin'. I'll see you later."

"Maybe," said Cyndi, smiling and looking up from her paper work.

ooooo

Bill Buttermore got into his brown, 1985 Crown Victoria and headed towards Beaufort. On the way, he stopped for a cup of coffee and a restroom break, and read the details of the trooper's report. He read that the ambulance had been southbound on Old Sheldon Church Road. The trooper's diagram showed that the accident had taken place south of Cotton Hall Road, an area which he knew well. He thought to himself that it would be best to video the approach to the site in the same direction that the ambulance had taken. From Yemassee, he began to drive on Old Sheldon Church Road. "When did this new pavement get put down?" he thought to himself. When he arrived at the intersection of Old Sheldon Church Road and Cotton Hall Road, he turned on his emergency flashers and pulled off into the gore area where the two roads met at a shallow angle. Grabbing the video camera, his clipboard, measuring tape, and measuring wheel, he walked south on Old Sheldon Church Road in the shoulder area. He noted, measured, photographed, and took video of the fresh markings on the pavement edge and shoulder where the ambulance left the road. From the surface of the new asphalt to the surface of the grassy shoulder was six inches. As he wrote in his notebook, he thought to himself, "This is no good." He looked towards the northbound lane of Old Sheldon Church Road. "Where's the new pavement for that lane?" he thought to himself. He walked several hundred feet more to the south; video-documenting the evidence that the ambulance followed the curvature of the road for approximately fifty feet before attempting to reenter the road. At that point, he measured the drop-off from the surface of the new pavement to the shoulder: eight inches. "Wow," he thought. As he continued to walk along the pavement, he noted the rubbing of the tire and the crumbling of the asphalt edge, which extended for approximately one hundred feet. The crumbling stopped where the right front tire had finally grabbed the road. The marks on the road clearly showed the turning of the ambulance into the northbound lane, the sudden turn right turn to miss the oncoming truck, and where the ambulance had fallen onto its side and skidded into the oak tree. Bill was standing there, taking pictures and video of the marks on the oak tree, when he smelled the distinct odor of an asphalt paving operation. A dump truck with fresh asphalt passed by in the southbound lane. He knew the smell very well because he had helped with traffic control on a few asphalt pavement jobs as a trooper. Bill knew that road contractors routinely used advance warning signs, barrels, and other traffic control devices during the asphalt paving, at both ends of a road open to traffic. Looking to the south, he saw a paving operation moving north in the northbound lane. "Well, what do we have here?" he said to himself. "I did not see any road construction signs or barrels when I came in from the north."

Bill took a few more photographs of the tree and then hid all of his equipment behind the tree, under some brush. He did not want to look like an investigator. Then he walked toward the paving operation. He saw how they were alternating north and southbound traffic in the southbound lane while paving the northbound lane. Bill walked further south and noticed a truck parked on the northbound shoulder. The sign on the side of the truck said, "BISHOP CONSTRUCTION COMPANY."

Bill walked up to the truck on the driver's side and nodded at the driver. Trevor Arnold, who was reading the Red Book when he felt someone next to his window, looked up. "Can I help, you?" said Trevor in a startled tone.

"I'm not sure," said Bill. "My name is Bill Buttermore. What is your name?"

"I'm Trevor Arnold. There's a lot of equipment rolling around. You should not be here."

"I know," said Bill, in a very conciliatory tone. "I apologize for being here. Did you hear about the accident with the ambulance down the road?"

"Yes, I did. It was a sad thing to happen. Why do you ask?"

"A friend of the family asked me to come here and see if there was anything to gather up," which, while not completely accurate, wasn't technically a lie. Not wanting Trevor to take control of the conversation, Bill asked, "Have you found anything since the accident, personal belongings and such?"

"No, not a thing," said Trevor.

"Good. How long you guys been out here?" said Bill.

"A little over two weeks," said Trevor.

"Are there any other road contractors I can speak to?" said Bill.

"No, we're it. You might want to ask anybody in a SCDOT truck. They might be able to help," said Trevor.

"Thanks. I appreciate your help," said Bill, shaking Trevor's hand.

Trevor watched Bill walk to the other side of the road and turn north.

"That was odd," thought Trevor to himself. He had heard from a friend about how there was a pregnant girl involved in the accident, and that a doctor was hurt real bad. His stomach started to hurt, just below the sternum.

Bill began his walk back to his car. He crossed back over Old Sheldon Church Road and walked north on the southbound shoulder, thinking to himself, "We have a newly-paved road, the contractor is Bishop Construction Company, and it is a SCDOT project." He gathered his equipment from behind the tree, and continued toward his car, once again passing the pavement edge to his right, and thought, "Eight inches, really?" He looked up to the north and saw no barrels or signs. He thought about the roadway safety seminar he had mentioned to Cephas Hampton earlier. "There is something wrong here," he said to himself. "What was that instructor's name?"

ooooo

Monday morning, Bill Buttermore walked into the law office at nine o'clock. After a minute of pleasantries with Cyndi Carday, he walked up to the entrance of Cephas' office and knocked on the open door.

Cephas looked up and said, "Hey. How'd it go Friday?"

"I think we may have something here," said Bill.

He went on to explain to Cephas about the shoulder drop-off, the crumbling edge of the asphalt pavement, how the north and southbound lanes of Old Sheldon Church Road were being repaved by Bishop

Construction Company, and the involvement of the SCDOT. He further explained how he had approached the incident scene from the same direction as the ambulance; but saw no warning signs, barrels or anything else to let a driver know they were approaching a construction zone.

"Assuming I can get all the parties in the ambulance to sign on as clients, what do you think we need to do next?" said Cephas.

"Remember that roadway safety seminar in Atlanta I mentioned? The instructor who talked about construction signage, the dangers of shoulder drop-offs, and other safety topics was a man named Allen Sterling. We should have him look at this and get his thoughts on what could have been done to prevent the accident."

"Where's he located?" said Cephas.

"He's an assistant professor at Georgia Tech. He's also a licensed professional engineer. And from what I heard from him, he can rub two sentences together," said Bill.

"Sounds good. I like it that he's out of state, but not too far. He probably won't be influenced by the SCDOT or anyone else in South Carolina," said Cephas. "You have his number?"

"I'm going to look it up when I get home," said Bill.

"Tell you what," said Cephas. "I want you to call Mr. Sterling and see if he's available. Find out his hourly rates, his retainer requirement, and anything else he might need. While you do that, I am going to set up a meeting this week with Maurice and the Jesup family. If the Jesup family signs on as a client, I'll see if the others will sign on as well. Good work, Brother Bill."

"No problem," said Bill, as he turned and left.

After Bill left, Cephas picked up and dialed his desk phone. "Maurice, this is Cephas. You got a minute?"

"Hey, Cephas. Of course I've got a minute. What did you find out?"

"There may be a case here," said Cephas. "In fact, there may be a big case. My man, Bill Buttermore, told me there are some real problems that could have been prevented. Do you think I could come to Beaufort the day after tomorrow and meet with you and the Jesup family that evening?"

"I think that would be fine," said Dr. Honeycutt. "I will call Christine's daddy to set it up."

"Perfect," said Cephas. "Please let them know that I will be bringing paperwork to sign them up as a client. I will also set it up so that Mr. Jesup can sign for Christine. If they ask you, and people usually do, please stress that this will cost them nothing. Any expenses up to, and including, a trial will be paid for by me. I only get paid if there is a settlement or judgment in their favor. While I will go over it again when we meet, I believe they will be more at ease if it initially comes from you. Don't you think?"

"I do," said Dr. Honeycutt. "Thank you for jumping on this so quickly, Cephas."

"You're welcome, Cuz. Call me when you know something."

"Will do," said Dr. Honeycutt.

ooooo

After leaving Cephas' office, Bill went back to his home office and looked up the classroom documents he had received from the seminar he attended in Atlanta. He found the contact information for Allen Sterling, and called him.

"Hello?" said Mr. Sterling.

"Mr. Sterling, this is a former student of yours, Bill Buttermore. Well, I am not really a student, but one of the attendees at your road safety seminar in Atlanta a while back."

"Well, Mr. Buttermore," said Mr. Sterling in a joking tone, "please accept my apology for not remembering you. In any event, how can I help?"

"No problem," said Bill with a smile. "I work as an investigator for an attorney named Cephas Hampton in Columbia, South Carolina. I think we have a case where we'll need your help."

Bill told Mr. Sterling about what had happened to the ambulance. He told him about Christine Jesup's injuries, the lack of signage, and the condition of the pavement edge where the ambulance tried to reenter the roadway. He told him about the roadway contractor and the involvement of the SCDOT.

"Do you know what roadway specification was in effect?" said Mr.

38

Sterling
    "No, I don't," said Bill. Is that important?"

    "Very," said Mr. Sterling. "It is part of the contract between the SCDOT and the contractor that outlines the contractor's responsibilities with regard to public safety and the actual road construction. Speaking of road construction, tell me again about what you saw at the pavement edge."

Bill told Mr. Sterling that Cephas had not yet signed the clients. They made tentative arrangements to meet on a Saturday, which was necessary for two reasons. The first was that a Saturday would not interfere with Mr. Sterling's classroom schedule. Secondly, traffic was lighter on Old Sheldon Church Road on the weekends. Mr. Sterling would take care of getting the company to take the asphalt cores from the road. Bill would take care of having troopers on site to help with traffic control while the cores were being taken. Bill would make sure that one of the troopers attending would be Trooper Steven McPherson, who had completed the incident report.

    "Mr. Sterling, don't pull the trigger just yet," said Bill. "Once Cephas signs up the clients, we will send you your retainer, the trooper's report, a video taken of the scene, and anything else we gather in the meantime. While we are waiting, could you send me your *curriculum vitae?*"

    "Of course," said Mr. Sterling. "Just let me know when to start."

    "No problem. I will be talking with you soon," said Bill. "Thank you and goodbye, Mr. Sterling."

    "Goodbye, sir," said Allen.

8 - THE PLAINTIFF'S EXPERT WITNESS

Allen Peter Sterling, PE was different than most of his relatives in that his family was mostly blue collar. Except for his aunt on his father's side, he had been the first to receive a college degree. His father was a union carpenter who eventually owned his own non-union ceiling and drywall company. He started working for his father at the age of seven. He would sweep floors, pick up trash, and do anything else that a young boy could do. In the beginning, he was paid with snacks and Coca-Colas. That eventually had to change. During his high school years, he always worked for his father during the holiday and summer breaks. While not afraid of hard work, he knew he wanted to do something more with his life.

After high school, Mr. Sterling enrolled in the civil engineering department at the Georgia Institute of Technology in Atlanta. After his sophomore year, he decided to enroll in the cooperative education program at Georgia Tech. This program allowed students to alternate work and school by going to school one quarter, and working for a company in their chosen field the next quarter. Allen's co-op was with the Georgia Department of Transportation (GADOT). Initially, he worked with field crews inspecting road and bridge construction in the immediate Atlanta area. His jobs were many. He took cores for asphalt testing, checked roadway alignment, verified pay items and quantities turned in by the roadway contractors, and inspected the placement of temporary signage and barrels in the construction zones.

After receiving his Bachelor of Science degree in civil engineering, Allen went to work full time for the GADOT as a roadway designer. At his first opportunity, he took, and passed, the first of two eight-hour tests to become a licensed professional engineer (PE). This test was known as the Engineer in Training, or EIT, exam. In addition to working for four years under the guidance of PE's at the GADOT, Mr. Sterling completed his master's degree in civil engineering at Georgia Tech. Upon graduation, he accepted a position as an assistant professor, and was a doctoral candidate at Georgia Tech. While it was not necessary for an academic position, he took and passed the final eight-hour test to become a licensed engineer.

Because he wrote many peer-reviewed articles and papers, and co-authored many books on roadway construction safety, he was sought after as a seminar speaker on the subject. In addition, he had been retained by several plaintiff and defense attorneys as a consultant and expert witness on legal cases involving accidents in roadway construction zones.

9 - THE BATTLE BEGINS

With Maurice's convincing, Cephas gained Christine Jesup as a client. Over the next few days, he also signed up Betty Pitts, Gerald Toombs, and Maggie Bunn. Even though the injuries to each person were from the same incident, each client's injuries differed in severity. Because of this, Cephas decided that each client's lawsuit should be filed separately. Bill Buttermore found the corporate address for Bishop Construction Company in Beaufort. In one day, all four lawsuits were filed in Beaufort County, and were delivered, certified mail, to Nathan Bishop's office. In each lawsuit, it stated that "the actions of defendant Bishop Construction Company, or its agents, caused the injuries to the plaintiff." The lawsuit further stated that "the plaintiff demands a jury trial to determine actual and punitive damages to be paid by the defendant."

While the lawsuit filings were being completed and served, Allen Sterling was given the green light to begin his investigation. Bill Buttermore sent him a copy of the video taken at the incident scene, the trooper's incident report, and photographs he had taken. From these items, Mr. Sterling developed a list of documents and other items to request from Bishop Construction Company. They included the contract between Bishop and the SCDOT, plans and specifications for the asphalt overlay project on Old Sheldon Church Road, asphalt testing results, and any correspondence between Nathan Bishop and the SCDOT.

ooooo

"I did nothing wrong!" screamed Nathan Bishop to Byron Heard over the telephone. "These lawsuits are crap. They are just a bunch of people trying to make me pay for their misfortune. My crew was on the other end of the road when the accident occurred. How is this my fault?"

"Nathan, you have two injured EMT's, a traumatized pregnant teenager, and a quadriplegic doctor, all of whom were injured on a road you were working on. The perception is pretty bad," said Byron. "The first thing you need to do is send those lawsuits to your insurance company. Who is your liability insurance company, anyway?"

...to be made whole again.

"Fidelis Mutual," said Nathan.

"Good," said Byron. "I have worked with them before. They will let me be your attorney for this. Get those lawsuits in today."

10 - THE DEFENSE

Fidelis Mutual was a relative newcomer to the insurance market in South Carolina. It had started out selling property insurance in 1980. At the time, South Carolina was a very lucrative state to do business. In eight years, Fidelis' marketing activities allowed them to acquire an almost forty percent market share in South Carolina. Then, in 1989, Hurricane Hugo came to Charleston and the Low Country of South Carolina. While the storm surge from Hugo allowed Fidelis Mutual to deny many property claims due to the flooding exclusion, there was no denying the claims for wind damage to the thousands of inland properties. Hundreds of millions of dollars were paid out to cover the thousands of property claims. After Hugo, Fidelis Mutual decided to stop selling property insurance policies in South Carolina. Instead, they decided to sell general liability policies to high-risk construction companies. High-risk construction companies paid much higher premiums, which made the profit margin much higher. There were many reasons that would make a construction company qualify in that category. In the case of their policy holder Bishop Construction Company, being forbidden from bidding on roadway projects. But, given that they were now allowed to bid, and that the company had been in business for many decades, they had been deemed an acceptable risk.

"Byron Heard, please," said Shirley Stone.
"One moment, please," said his receptionist.

Shirley Stone, executive vice president at Fidelis Mutual, was not used to holding on for people to answer the telephone. After about fifteen seconds, her frustration changed to amusement when she thought about how things were always slower in the South.

"This is Byron Heard."
"Mr. Heard, this is Shirley Stone with Fidelis Mutual in New York. I need to speak with you about several lawsuits we just received from South Carolina. We may need your help."
"Yes, ma'am," he said.
"Our legal department recommended you for our local counsel

because you have worked for us in the past. They also said that our insured, Nathan Bishop, is, pardon the expression, a regular client of yours. Is that true?" said Ms. Stone.

"It is, ma'am," he said thinking that last remark was a little rude. "I have worked for Nathan Bishop for many years. In fact, I have already reviewed the demand letters from each of the plaintiffs. I suggested that Nathan get all those documents to you as soon as possible."

"Great," she said. "We would like to retain you. What are your initial thoughts on settling all these cases? We only have one million to work with. I would like for all of these to settle for much less."

"One million dollars?" asked Byron. "Have you read the demand letters?"

"Of course I have," she said. From what I read, you have a teenaged mother from a very poor family who probably never saw a hundred dollar bill before, two EMT's with a broken bone, and a hurt doctor. The teenager's family will probably take the first offer we make. The EMT's have health insurance where they work and will take a check for about two years' salary, and the doctor will take the rest. Is there a problem?"

"The doctor is a quadriplegic," said Byron. "It may take more for her."

"We don't have more," said Ms. Stone, sounding disgusted. "One million is all we have, and one million is all these people are going to get. And besides, it remains to be seen if the doctor is actually a quad. She might be faking."

"Faking?" said Byron. "I guess we'll find out pretty soon."

"I mean no disrespect," said Ms. Stone thinking many such thoughts with a smile on her face. "But the South is known for frivolous personal injury lawsuits. Fidelis is not going to buy into it any longer."

"I understand," said Byron. He thought to himself, "I *understand* that I am about to get involved with a real sweetheart of a person."

"Good," said Ms. Stone. "Let's get these settled quickly."

"Yes, ma'am," said Byron. Privately, he thought that he would not feel too bad about billing five hundred hours per lawsuit.

"Goodbye," she said thinking how quaint it was that all southern men had such good manners.

11 - MATERIAL TESTING

After Allen Sterling reviewed the notes, photographs, and video sent to him by Bill Buttermore, a day was set up for the inspection of the incident scene. Bill Buttermore coordinated traffic control with the local state troopers. Mr. Sterling arranged for a coring company to be on site to take asphalt cores from the road.

The day started at eight o'clock on Saturday morning. Everyone met at the intersection of Old Sheldon Church Road and Cotton Hall Road. With the help of Trooper Steven McPherson, Mr. Sterling noted the location of where the ambulance left the road, and where it had tried to remount the road. It was starting at the remount point where cores were going to be taken for testing. Three locations, approximately one hundred feet apart, were chosen. Five cores, each with a six inch diameter, were taken at each location. The amount of asphalt to be taken for testing, and the testing itself, was determined by the national standards published by the American Society for Testing and Materials (ASTM). Each set of five cores, one set from each of the five locations, was wrapped in plastic and placed in a box. The boxes were labeled A, B, and C, respectively. In the job notebook, Mr. Sterling noted the distance from the stop sign at Cotton Hall Road to each of the three locations. The stop sign was a common reference point in the incident report and in the notebooks of Mr. Sterling and Bill Buttermore. After all the cores were taken, and the holes created by the coring were filled with asphalt, Mr. Sterling took possession of the three boxes. As it was Saturday, he took them back to his home until he could deliver them to the testing laboratory on Monday morning. Mr. Sterling thought about taking them to Georgia Tech for testing; but decided against it because this was a private matter, and the equipment at Georgia Tech was public property.

On Monday morning, Mr. Sterling delivered the three boxes of asphalt cores to Harry Corn of PST Laboratories. During his co-op time at the GADOT, Mr. Sterling had met Mr. Corn. Roadway contractors would hire PST to perform the required quality control testing, while Mr. Sterling, for the GADOT, would perform the quality assurance testing for comparison.

They had met several times in the past to discuss any discrepancies between their asphalt test results. Mr. Sterling had come to know Harry Corn as someone he could trust.

Allen Sterling pulled to the back of the offices of PST where deliveries were made. He backed up to the bumper guards at a delivery door. Walking up the short, metal industrial stairs, he opened the metal door and proceeded to Harry Corn's office, as he had done dozens of times before. He knocked on Mr. Corn's open door.

"What are you reading, Harry?" said Mr. Sterling.

Harry looked up from the test report he was proofreading and said, "Well, look what the cat dragged in. How are you, Allen?"

"I'm fine. How's the testing business?" said Mr. Sterling.

"About the same," said Harry. It's either feast or famine. Did you bring those asphalt cores we talked about?"

"Sure did," said Mr. Sterling. "They're in my car parked in the back. Let's go take a look at them."

Mr. Sterling brought in the three boxes and placed them on a work table. The asphalt cores were taken out and placed in three piles, each core labeled by location.

"Harry, I need you to cut off the top layer on each core. Combine the cores as run tests on each of the three locations," said Mr. Sterling.

"What tests do you want run?" said Harry.

"I need the percentage of asphalt, gradation of the aggregate, angularity of the larger aggregate, density of the core, and type of bitumen," said Mr. Sterling.

"What are you looking for?" asked Harry.

"I am not sure," said Mr. Sterling. "When I went to the accident site, I noticed that the tire trying to get back onto the road caused the asphalt to crumble like a dry cake mix. Something is going on, I am just not quite sure what."

"Understood," said Harry. "If I see any abnormalities, I will call you."

"Great," said Mr. Sterling. "Don't forget to include the certification and calibration certificates in the final report."

"I won't," said Harry. "Thanks for the business."

"No problem," said Mr. Sterling.

PST was a national testing firm which tested asphalt, concrete, and other construction materials for clients throughout the United States. It was important to PST to achieve consistent and reproducible testing results if the same materials were tested by another laboratory. To accomplish this, specifically with asphalt materials, the technicians were certified through the Asphalt Institute. In addition, all the devices used to weigh or provide other forms of measurement were calibrated through the National Institute of Standards and Technology (NIST), formally known as the National Bureau of Standards. PST would bring in calibration companies whose calibration equipment could be traced back to NIST standards.

ooooo

After two weeks, the tests performed by PST were completed. Harry Corn was sitting at his desk when the telephone rang.

"This is Harry."

"Harry, this is Allen. How is it going? Any news?"

"I was just thinking about you. You must have been reading my mind. I just so happen to have the results in my hands right now," said Harry.

"Well, what's the verdict?"

"The densities turned out ok. The size and distribution of the fine and course aggregate were ok. The problem is the percentage of dust and the percentage of asphalt," said Harry.

"What do you mean?"

"Every job mix formula I have ever seen requires a dust-to-asphalt ratio between 0.6 and 1.2. These dust and asphalt amounts put this mix at a minimum of 1.3."

"Wow," said Mr. Sterling. "That makes for a real dry mix. You know why this usually happens?"

"Yeah, and you do too," said Harry. "Money. Dust is cheap and asphalt is expensive. More dust and less asphalt means a cheaper price per ton of asphalt mix."

"When will your formal report be ready?" said Mr. Sterling.

...to be made whole again.

"By end of business tomorrow," said Harry.

"Good. I look forward to getting it. Please make three copies. I will need one for me, one for my client, and one for him to send to the defense attorney."

"Will do," said Harry. "I'll talk with you later."

"See you later," said Mr. Sterling.

12 - THE BIRTH OF OPINIONS

During the two weeks it had taken to obtain the test results from PST, Allen Sterling received and reviewed the documents he had requested from Cephas Hampton. Cephas had prepared a "Request for Documents" letter for Byron Heard. Byron's staff went to the Yard and met with Trevor Arnold to get them together. Nathan Bishop would have nothing to do with this because he thought it was a complete waste of time. Copies were made and sent to Cephas' office which, in turn, sent copies to Mr. Sterling. These documents contained the contract between Bishop and the SCDOT, plans and specifications for the asphalt overlay project on Old Sheldon Church Road, asphalt testing results, and all correspondence between Bishop and the SCDOT. The contract documents between the SCDOT and Bishop Construction Company plainly stated that "all the work shall be in conformance to any prepared construction plans, and the 1986 Edition of the SCDOT Standard Specifications for Highway Construction," – the Red Book.

"Mr. Hampton, this is Allen Sterling. Do you have a moment to talk?"

"Mr. Sterling, I'll always have a moment to speak with you. What's up?" said Cephas.

"The asphalt test results are back. I have reviewed the construction plans and specifications, the contract between the SCDOT, and the Red Book. There is ample evidence that the actions, or should I say inactions, of Bishop Construction, were the cause of the ambulance incident," said Mr. Sterling.

"What do you mean?" said Cephas.

Mr. Sterling told Cephas about the problems with the asphalt which caused it to crumble under the weight of the ambulance tire. He told him about the contractual responsibilities of Bishop Construction Company to the traveling public regarding signage and safety.

"Mr. Sterling, based on what you have told me, I am going to name you as our expert witness," said Cephas. "Before I do that, I will need an expert affidavit from you outlining your opinions in this case. Normally, I would not need this from an expert, but given the technical nature of this case, the other side is going to have to hire an engineering expert to defend. I will have my people send you over the front and end portions of a generic affidavit. You will need to fill in the middle portion, sign it in front of a notary, and send me the original. Any questions?"

"No questions," said Mr. Sterling. "This is pretty straightforward stuff. Let me know if more documents come in, or if there are any changes in the case."

"Will do," said Cephas. "Talk to you soon."

13 - AN EXPERT FOR THE DEFENSE

Byron Heard was sitting at his desk the next morning after receiving a letter from Cephas Hampton, and an affidavit from his expert, Allen Sterling. "Who is Allen Sterling?" he thought to himself. He picked up the telephone and called Professor Thaddeus A. Thomas, PhD, at the University of Alabama College of Engineering. Dr. Thomas was the director of the Materials Testing Department, where he taught many courses on asphalt, concrete, soils, and other materials used in roadway and building construction. Byron had used Dr. Thomas on several lawsuits in which the quality of the construction materials was in question. Dr. Thomas was very popular with cost-conscious defense clients in the southeastern United States. With the use of university owned equipment, and the free labor provided by more than eager undergraduate and graduate students, he was able to pass along the savings to his clients.

"Dr. Thomas, this is Byron Heard, from Columbia, South Carolina. How are you doing today?"

"I am fine, Mr. Heard," said Dr. Thomas. "What is it that you need?" He thought to himself that attorneys were always calling him because they needed something.

"Dr. Thomas," said Byron. "I have a case I need your help with. I am working for the insurance company that insures a roadway contractor, the defendant. It is alleged by the plaintiff's expert that there are problems with the construction signage, and the asphalt mix. They..."

Dr. Thomas cut him off. "Who is the plaintiff's expert?"

"Allen Sterling," said Byron.

"Allen Sterling?" said Dr. Thomas. "I have never heard of him. What does he know about asphalt and construction signage?"

"He is an associate professor at Georgia Tech. He teaches roadway construction and safety."

"An *associate* professor?" Dr. Thomas thought to himself. "This will be easy." To Byron, he said, "What work has he performed on this case, so far?"

"We have asphalt testing results, and we have his affidavit," said Byron.

"What kind of asphalt project was it?" asked Dr. Thomas.

"The defendant was placing a two inch overlay on an existing road," said Byron. "An ambulance flipped over in the construction zone."

"Have your defendant scrape off about two pounds of new asphalt and send it to me," said Dr. Thomas. "I will have it tested here at my lab. Where is the nearest major airport to the accident scene?"

"Columbia," said Byron.

"Have someone from your office available to pick me up at the airport and take me to the accident site," said Dr. Thomas. "I will call you with a date and time. Even though it is truly unnecessary for me to see the scene to render an opinion, it must be done. In the meantime, send me the affidavit of the esteemed Allen Sterling, plus any photographs you might have. Oh – do not forget the retainer check to cover my time and asphalt testing."

"I won't," said Byron. I will send you those things tomorrow."

"Good," said Dr. Thomas as he hung up the telephone.

Dr. Thomas sat back in his chair and thought to himself how these cases had always been lucrative. With his opinion backed by a PhD, the free use of the testing equipment, and the free labor of his students, he figured they would never end.

ooooo

Thaddeus Thomas came from a well-educated family. His mother and father had PhD's in child psychology and chemistry, respectively. His two older sisters had advanced degrees – one in music, the other in social work. Higher education was the unspoken family business. Because of his parents' connections to the local universities and the corporations that always wanted to do business at these universities, the Thomas family always had memberships to play at the local golf courses and other entertainment venues. Rather than his father taking the time to teach Thaddeus how to perform home or car maintenance, minor construction, or anything else men normally teach their sons, Thaddeus learned how to "country club." He was very good at it.

When the time came for Thaddeus to decide on a career, he thought about how much fun he had had playing in the dirt as a boy when his parents were not looking. "Civil engineers play in the dirt, so that must be the job for me!" was pretty much how the decision was made. At the beginning of his junior year, he realized that if he were to become an actual engineer, he might have to get a job where he would have to design something. It was at that time he decided to become a professor. This way, he could work in the civil engineering profession without ever having to do actual civil engineering work. Never having to take a private sector job during college, or ever, for that matter, Thaddeus went straight through college to receive his bachelors, masters, and doctorate degrees. After receiving his PhD at the age of thirty, he accepted a position at the University of Alabama as their Director of Materials and Testing. For twenty years he had held that position with unquestioned authority over the equipment in his labs, and the students in his classes.

14 - THE DEPOSITIONS

During the discovery period of a lawsuit, both sides are required by law to produce all documents they plan to use at trial, even if the ultimate plan is to settle without a trial. There can be no surprises. The judge will throw out any evidence introduced that could have been introduced during the discovery period. Each side will ask the other to produce documents relevant to the case. These documents may include the names of all people who have knowledge of the incident at hand. In the case of Bishop Construction, the most knowledgeable person was Trevor Arnold. Both Nathan Bishop and Trevor Arnold were subpoenaed for deposition. In addition, the expert witnesses for each side are named. The expert witness named for the plaintiff was Allen P. Sterling, PE. The expert named for the defense was Thaddeus A. Thomas, PhD. Because the plaintiff's expert usually develops his opinions first, he is usually the first expert to be deposed. In most legal text books, the stated purpose of the expert deposition is for the other side to find out as much as they can about the opposing expert. Where does he live? Does he have relatives in the venue where the trial may take place? Where did he go to school? What are his opinions? What materials did he use to develop his opinions? The other purpose of the expert deposition is to find the chinks in the expert's armor? Those questions are sometimes a little more subtle.

ooooo

The depositions of Nathan Bishop and Trevor Arnold were taken in the conference room at Byron Heard's office. Nathan Bishop's was taken first. It became quickly apparent to Cephas Hampton that this was almost a waste of time, in that with every question asked, Nathan always deferred to Trevor. Trevor Arnold did this. Trevor Arnold did that. Nathan Bishop may as well have said that with the exception of writing the payroll checks, Trevor Arnold ran Bishop Construction Company. Byron sat there and never made any objections or asked any questions. His demeanor gave the impression that he was satisfied with the training he had given Nathan.

Nathan's deposition ended at 11:45 am. They decided to take a lunch break and reconvene at 1:30. Byron, Nathan, and Trevor walked across the street to a sandwich shop.

After getting their lunches cafeteria-style, Nathan looked at Trevor and said, "Trevor, Byron and I have some talking to do. Could you sit over there while we talk?"

"Sure," said Trevor. "I'll be just right over here." He walked away to a table near the front window of the restaurant, sitting down at a two-person table with a view of the street. As he ate his sandwich, the thought about how this was going to be his first deposition. "What will he ask me? What if I don't answer right?"

Byron and Nathan took a table at the back of the restaurant, far away from any prying ears.

"What do you think Trevor is going to say?" said Byron.

"He'll say whatever we tell him to," said Nathan. "Remember this: he still wants a job. He will deliver."

"How can you be so sure? You do understand that he could potentially sink this case?" said Byron. "He was out there every day. Yours and Trevor's testimony must be consistent. Cephas Hampton will take advantage of any inconsistency."

"Don't you worry about Trevor. He will say what is needed," said Nathan.

Byron leaned forward to eat more of his lunch. He thought it better not to ask what Nathan meant.

ooooo

At 1:35 pm. the deposition of Trevor Arnold began.

Cephas Hampton said, "This shall be the deposition of Trevor Arnold for the purposes of discovery. It is stipulated that this deposition is taken pursuant to Notice of Taking Deposition and/or agreement of counsel, yet all question as to sufficiency of such notice or agreement is waived; that all objections, except as to the form of the question, are reserved until the time of trial. Does the witness want to read and sign?"

"What does that mean?" said Trevor.

"You have the right to read your deposition and make any corrections," said Cephas.

"I guess I want to read and sign," said Trevor.

"Good," said Cephas. Court reporter, please swear in the witness."

"Sir, please raise your right hand," said the court reporter. Trevor complied.

"Do you solemnly swear that the testimony you are about to give will be the truth, the whole truth, and nothing but the truth, so help you God?" said the court reporter.

"I do," said Trevor.

Examination by Mr. Hampton

Q   Please state your full name for the record.

A   Trevor James Arnold

Q   Mr. Arnold, have you ever given a deposition before?

A   No.

Q   I understand. There are a few things I need you to remember while we do this. Basically, I will ask questions, and you will answer them. I ask that you answer with a "yes" or "no." If you only shake your head, the court reported cannot tell what your answer is. Also, please allow me to finish my question before you answer. If you start talking before the question is completed, the court reporter may not hear the whole question. Understand?

A   Yes sir.

Q   Mr. Arnold, I only ask you this next question because it is your first deposition. Do you know what perjury is?

A   No, sir.

Q   Perjury is the offense of lying under oath. You have raised your right
     hand and sworn an oath to tell the truth to the court. If it were
     discovered that your answers to my questions were not truthful, you
     could be found guilty of perjury. If you were found guilty of perjury,
     you may have to pay a fine and possibly do jail time. Do you
     understand?

By Mr. Heard: Are you finished scaring the witness?

By Mr. Hampton: Scaring the witness? Byron, obviously I'm just doing the
job you should have done.

Q   Mr. Arnold, did you understand me?

A   Yes, sir.

At that moment, Trevor had never been more scared in his life. He
thought, "Pay a fine? Go to jail? No job is worth that."

Q   Good. Where do you live?

For the next 45 minutes, Cephas Hampton established that Trevor Arnold
had been a lifelong resident of Beaufort County, was a high school dropout,
and had a juvenile record. Trevor answered truthfully that he had been
charged with petty theft when he was fourteen years old. He told Cephas
that he had stolen a neighbor boy's bicycle on a dare from a pretty girl. The
pretty girl had wanted to get back at the boy for breaking up with her. As it
turned out, the neighbor boy was the son of a policeman. As Trevor
explained the charge, Cephas thought to himself, "What pretty girls can
make boys do."

Q   Have you committed any other crimes against humanity? (Cephas had
     a friendly smile on his face.)

A   No sir, that is all.

Q   I see. How long have you been with Bishop Construction?

A   A little over seven years.

Q   You were the Project Manager for Bishop Construction Company during the asphalt   overlay project on Old Sheldon Church Road, correct?

A   That is correct.

Q   Tell me about your responsibilities as project manager.

A   I was responsible for the day-to-day activities of the crews. I made sure the asphalt was delivered. I made sure it was placed. I made sure the asphalt got tested as required by the SCDOT. I placed, or directed those that placed, the warning signage and barrels in the work zone.

Q   Let's talk about your asphalt testing.

Cephas asked many questions about the asphalt testing performed by Trevor Arnold. Byron thought to himself, "If he wants to waste his time going down this rabbit trail, it's his own time to waste."

Q   Who approved the equipment you used for the asphalt testing?

A   People from the district engineer's office came. They also inspected the equipment.

Q   Is Drew Richards in charge of that office?

A   Yes, he is.

Q   What did they do to inspect the equipment? Were you there?

A   I was there. They inspected the equipment to make sure it was clean. They brought some weights to put on our scales to see if they were accurate.

Q   So the SCDOT certified your equipment?

A   Yes.

Q   Do you know if the SCDOT has their equipment certified or calibrated?

A   I don't know anything about that.

Q   Good enough. Photographs taken the day of the incident have established that there were no warning signs or barrels in the vicinity of where the ambulance wreck occurred. Why were there no warning signs or barrels?

A   We did have warning signs and barrels. We always use warning signs and barrels. It is required by the roadway specifications. They were there.

Cephas thought that this response was a little too formal – too rehearsed.

Q   Where were they?

A   They were at the location of the work.

Q   Where was the work on the date the incident occurred?

A   At the south end of Old Sheldon Church Road.

Q   What about at the north end? How were the people traveling south going to know there was road construction work ahead?

A   The signs for "Construction Ahead" were closer to the actual work.

Q   Were you aware of the eight inch drop-off on the west side of the road?

A   I was aware of it, but I was told that we were not required to do anything about it.

Q   Who told you that you did not have to do anything about it?

A   There was nothing in the contract. There was nothing in the contract that said we had to do anything.

Q   That wasn't my question, Mr. Arnold. You said, "I was told that we were not required." I want to know who told you that you did not have to do anything about the eight inch drop-off.

A   The contract said so.

Rather than pulling the trigger on the "I am calling the judge" strategy, Cephas decided on a different tactic.

Q   Mr. Arnold, who is your direct supervisor or boss?

A   Nathan Bishop.

Q   Did Nathan Bishop tell you, as part of this project, that you did not have to do anything about the eight inch drop-off?

A   The contract said so.

Q   That was not my question. This is a "yes" or "no" question. You need to answer "yes" or "no". Did Nathan Bishop tell you that did not have to do anything about the eight inch drop-off?

    "Well, here it is," thought Trevor. "Here was the moment of truth, or lie, as the case may be. I don't want to go to jail. My cousins can get me a job in building construction."

A   Yes.

Q   And why did he tell you that?

A   Because it was not part of our contract.

Q   What about the part of the specifications where it states that the contractor shall maintain the road until the work is completed and accepted? Did you speak with each other about that?

A   We did.

Q   And what did Mr. Bishop tell you about that section?

A   It was his opinion that section only applied to the work he was being paid for.

Q   Did you and Mr. Bishop talk about alerting the engineer to the six inch drop-off?

A   We talked about it, but Nathan did not want to bring it up because of the cost to repair.

A great sense of relief fell over Trevor. He no longer felt obliged to cover for Nathan Bishop. The rest of the deposition was completed in about fifteen minutes.

ooooo

Two weeks later, it was morning at the law office of Cephas Hampton in Columbia. At the very end of a long conference table sat a court reporter, ready to take down the questions and answers during the deposition of Allen P. Sterling, PE. On one side of the table, near the end of the table, and closest to the windows sat Mr. Sterling and Cephas Hampton. On the other side of the table was Byron Heard. Byron was going through the file provided by Mr. Sterling. He took notes on what he saw so that he could ask questions about these documents later during the deposition. Cephas and Mr. Sterling sat quietly, waiting for Byron to finish. Cephas had spent the past two days preparing Mr. Sterling for this deposition. There was nothing else to discuss.

"Are we ready?" said Byron.
"I am ready," said Mr. Sterling.

Byron turned to look at the court reporter and said, "Let's begin."

Byron said, "This shall be the deposition of Allen P. Sterling for the purposes of discovery. It is stipulated that this deposition is taken pursuant to Notice of Taking Deposition and/or agreement of counsel, yet all question as to sufficiency of such Notice or agreement is waived; that all objections, except as to the form of the question, are reserved until the time of trial. Does the witness want to read and sign?"

"I want to read and sign," said Mr. Sterling.

"Good," said Byron. Court reporter, please swear in the witness."

"Do you solemnly swear that the testimony you are about to give will be the truth, the whole truth, and nothing but the truth, so help you God?" said the court reporter.

"I do," said Mr. Sterling.

Examination by Byron Heard

Q   Please state your full name and address for the record.

A   My name is Allen Peter Sterling.

For the first thirty minutes of the deposition, Byron asked about relatives, educational background, work history, and other general information.

Q   Mr. Sterling, you stated earlier that you have testified as an expert witness, correct?

A   That is correct.

Q   How many times have you testified at either deposition or at trial?

A   I have testified at one trial, one mediation, and several depositions. I cannot remember the exact number of depositions.

Q   What was the subject matter of these opportunities to testify?

A   Road cases. An incident occurred on a roadway where something about the road, or the signage, was at issue.

Q   I see. Have you given more than ten, or less than ten depositions?

A   I believe more than ten.

Q   Have you given more than twenty, or less than twenty depositions?

A   I believe it would be a little more than twenty.

Q   And of those twenty depositions, how many were for the plaintiff and how many were for the defense?

A   It is probably around a 50/50 split.

Q   Probably, you said. Probably. How come you do not know?

A   I've never really thought about it. I do get this question in deposition from time to time.

Q   If people are asking you this question, why do you not find out the answer? You keep notes, do you not?

A   The plaintiff/defense split does not matter to me.

Q   It does not matter? For your information, people ask you this question to find out if you are prone to support the plaintiff or defense. Now I will ask you again, how many plaintiff's cases and how many defense cases have you worked on?

Allen Sterling paused for a moment to think. He knew the deposition would not reflect a long, pregnant pause. He sat up in his chair, linked his fingers on the table, and began to speak.

A   I have no numbers for you Counselor. And, for the record, I have never supported the plaintiff or the defense in any case I have worked on. And, in the spirit of being clear, Mr. Hampton is an advocate for the plaintiff for this case. You are an advocate for the defense. I am an advocate for the truth, no matter which side I am working for.

By Mr. Heard: Objection. The witness' answer is non-responsive to the question.

By Mr. Hampton: The question was asked and answered, and pretty well, I might add.

Byron was livid. His face was red. Both of his hands were placed flat on the conference table. His eyes were fixed sternly on Mr. Sterling in an attempt to intimidate.

By Mr. Heard: No, it was not. The witness just stated that he gets this question, and I quote, "all the time." He knows the numbers, he is just not saying them.

By Mr. Hampton: Well, okay. Try your question again.

Q   Now, Mr. Sterling, please listen carefully. How many plaintiff's cases and how many defense cases have you worked on, and if you do not have numbers for each, do you work mostly for the plaintiff or for the defense?

A   The answer is the same, sir. It is about a 50/50 split.

Realizing that Mr. Sterling was not going to break on this point, Byron tried another tactic.

Q   I see. Well, do you have this information in your office?

A   I think so. It would take me some time to put it together.

Q   Good. Go back to your office and gather those numbers for me. Send me a letter with that information. Do you understand?

A   That will not be a problem. It will probably take me about a week's worth of time to compile the information. I will send you an invoice. I will need payment before I begin.

Q   Mr. Sterling, Mr. Hampton and I are officers of the court. You must comply with any reasonable request so that we can do our job. You must comply.

A   Yes, you are an officer of the court. But, you are not judge. And even a judge cannot make me work for free. You may have heard of the Thirteenth Amendment of the United States Constitution. It abolished slavery, did it not?

Realizing that this was going nowhere, Byron moved on.

Q   Fine. We'll take this up with the judge soon enough. You have opinions as to the cause of the accident we are here about, correct?

A   Correct.

Q   How many do you have?

A   Two.

Q   And what are those opinions?

A   My first opinion is that Bishop Construction violated the contract documents by not providing adequate signage and warning. My second opinion is that Bishop Construction violated the contract documents by not providing a proper asphalt mix. Both of my opinions represent a failure of the duties of the contractor to carry out the contract.

Instead of following up with Allen Sterling about the specifics of his opinions, Byron decided to redirect his thinking.

Q   I see. You mentioned that your father was in the ceiling and drywall business. Tell me about your work responsibilities with your father's company.

A   In the early years, I would help by sweeping the floors, collecting trash, and being a helper to the mechanics actually doing the work. Later on, I would actually install ceilings and drywall. I would do these things between quarters and on summer breaks.

Q   Did any of the skills and knowledge you gained while working with your father, a ceiling and drywall contractor, have anything to do with the opinions you have regarding the case you are here for today?

While this question may seem ridiculous, it was very intentional. It was asked so that Mr. Sterling would think it *was* ridiculous. The hope for this type of question is usually to irritate the expert, to wear him down, and to make him less mentally sharp.

Mr. Sterling sat quietly for a second. "Why is he asking this question?" he asked himself.

A   The only skill and knowledge I bring from those days to this case is a good work ethic.

Q   That's it?

(Byron said this with a hint of sarcasm.)

A   Isn't that enough, Mr. Heard? You make a good work ethic sound like a bad thing.

(Byron was not pleased with this smart aleck answer.)

Q   Mr. Sterling, may I remind you how this works here today? I ask the questions. You answer them. Do you understand?

A   My apologies, Mr. Heard (said most insincerely). What you may hear as disrespect in my voice is actually confusion. I was confused as to why you would bring up my ceiling and drywall experience during a case involving roadway construction.

Q I decide what questions to ask. Again, I ask you, do you understand?

A I understand, completely. It is all very clear.

Q Are those two opinions your only opinions in this case?

A Based on the current evidence, those are my only opinions at this time.

Q Let's start with your first opinion. What specific section of the contract documents was violated regarding signage?

A Section 104.06 of the Red Book. That section is entitled "Maintenance and Maintaining Traffic." I am going to read the sentence that I think is of interest here. "The contractor will be required without direct compensation to maintain in good condition and satisfactory of the engineer the entire section or sections of highway within the limits of the contract, for the time he first begins work until all work has been completed and accepted."

Q How did the contractor fail to maintain the condition of the roadway?

A By allowing there to be an excessive drop-off on the shoulder. It was neither fixed nor warned of. In other words, the contractor could have maintained it by bringing up the shoulder, or he had the option of simply warning against the hazard instead of fixing it, and the contractor did neither.

Q Do you know whether or not the highway department contracted with Bishop to bring in fill dirt to raise the shoulders, or to address them in any way?

A They did not.

Q Do you believe the SCDOT knew about the drop-off before the contract with Bishop Construction?

A   I do not know.

Q   Let's assume they did know. Why should Bishop be responsible for
     the shoulder drop-off if the highway department knew about it before
     the contract with Bishop Construction, and the means to correct the
     drop-off were not part of the contract with Bishop Construction?

A   Bishop had complete control of that section of the road. They were
     contractually, and in my opinion, morally, bound to fix the drop-off or
     warn of the drop-off. They did neither. Both Nathan Bishop and his
     project manager, Trevor Arnold, knew about the drop-off, but did
     nothing about it.

Q   How do you know they knew anything about it?

A   Mr. Arnold said so in his deposition.

Byron realized that Mr. Sterling was not going to concede anything on this
point. If anything, he had just given Cephas a catch phrase: "Mr. Arnold
said so."

Q   Let's talk about the asphalt mix. What, specifically, was wrong with
     the asphalt mix?

A   The dust-to-asphalt ratio was above the allowable limits.

Q   What are those limits?

A   The dust-to-asphalt ratio must be between 0.6 and 1.2. All asphalt
     samples tested were above 1.2.

Q   Let's talk about asphalt mixes in general. What are the different
     parameters that have to be met in an asphalt mix?

A   There are many. In no particular order of importance, there are the
     percentage of bitumen or liquid asphalt in the mix, the

gradation/distribution of the different sizes of sand, rock and dust in the mix, the dust-to-asphalt ratio, and the compaction of the mix. Those are the main ones in my mind. You also have to consider the type of liquid asphalt, and the shape of the aggregate.

Q   I see. Besides the dust-to-asphalt ratio you mentioned, was there anything else wrong with the asphalt mix?

A   There was not.

Q   So, with so many other parameters that were right about the asphalt mix, how can you say that this one thing, the dust-to-asphalt ratio, was contributory to this incident? We are talking about dust, for goodness' sakes.

A   We are talking about a mix. It is like making a cake from scratch. If one of the ingredients is not of good quality, or not the right amount, you ruin the cake.

Byron thought he had an opening to discredit, or at least rattle, Mr. Sterling.

Q   Cakes, Mr. Sterling? We are here about an incident in which Bishop Construction is accused of making Christine Jesup a quadriplegic, and you want to talk about cakes?

Seeing the theatrics in Byron's comments, Mr. Sterling did not get upset at this attempt to belittle his testimony.

A   Mr. Heard, my job as an expert is to educate. As you plainly said earlier, your job is to ask the questions. My job is to answer those questions with the assumption that you do not know the answer. I use analogies to accomplish this.

Q   Cakes, Mr. Sterling? (Byron shook his head left to right.) What about the dust-to-asphalt ratio contributed to this incident?

A   Because the dust-to-asphalt ratio was so high, the bond between the sand and stone was lessened.

Q   What evidence do you have of "lessened" bond?

A   The crumbling asphalt I saw when I performed my on-site visit to the incident scene. As the right tire was trying to gain traction on the shoulder drop-off, it was crumbling beneath the tire. Had the dust-to-asphalt ratio been proper, there most probably would have been a proper bond between the sand and stone to allow the tire to remount the road.

The rest of the deposition was uneventful. Byron would ask the same questions he had already asked five times before hoping for a different answer. He wanted to show any inconsistencies in Mr. Sterling's answers.

ooooo

Of the four lawsuits filed by Cephas Hampton, three settled out of court. EMT Betty Pitts, the driver of the ambulance who had broken her hip settled for $200,000. Gerald Toombs, the rider next to Ms. Pitts, settled for $100,000. His injuries were relatively minor compared to the others. He had only broken his forearm. Maggie Bunn settled for $200,000. She and her baby were fine. The only remaining lawsuit involved Christine Jesup. As a quadriplegic, her expenses had already been enormous, with more sure to follow. A medical consultant hired by Cephas estimated that it would take at least three million dollars to settle Christine's expenses and to provide for her future care.

ooooo

"I do not care what her current and future expenses will be," said Shirley Stone to Byron Heard over the telephone. "This was a one million dollar policy, and there is only $500,000 left. They will accept $200,000 now or this goes to trial."

"Ms. Stone, as your legal counsel in this matter," said Byron," I must remind you that they have demanded policy limits. We could settle this for $500,000. If this goes to trial, there could be punitive damages added to any verdict that…"

"Mr. Heard," she said, "you might not have heard me before. There will be no more offered at this time. Once in trial, we might offer an additional $200,000, but not before. I am, or should I say, we at Fidelis, are not going to pay any more than we have to, understood?"

"Understood, Ms. Stone," said Byron thinking to himself that he should have asked for a large retainer before taking this assignment.

"Good," she said. "Continue with the depositions and other discovery. Oh, Mr. Heard. You mentioned verdict. In South Carolina, for there to be a verdict, there has to be 100% agreement within the jury, correct?"

"That is correct," said Byron.

"All we need is one or more people to see this lawsuit for the fraud it is," said Ms. Stone. "Call me later."

ooooo

It was a Friday morning and Cephas was sitting at his desk reading the asphalt testing report prepared by Thaddeus A. Thomas, PhD. It was addressed to Byron Heard. He skipped to the "Conclusion" section, where it read,

> *"The asphalt mix placed by Bishop Construction Company on Old Sheldon Church Road is acceptable as specified by the job mix approved by the SCDOT. All parameters (i.e. percent asphalt, gradation of stone and sand, and DUST-TO-ASPHALT RATIO (emphasis added) are within the allowable limits."*

Cephas picked up his deck telephone and called Allen Sterling.

"Allen, this is Cephas in Columbia. How are you doing?"

"Fine," said Mr. Sterling. "What's the latest on our case?"

"Well, we may have a problem," said Cephas. "I have just read the asphalt test report from the lauded Thaddeus A. Thomas, PhD. Dr. Thomas has found that the asphalt mix placed by Bishop was perfect in every way."

"Interesting," said Mr. Sterling. "Did you really expect anything less?"

"No, but here is my problem," said Cephas. "Don't get me wrong. Your credentials are very good. However, we have a tenured, gray haired, well respected PhD from one of the most respected universities in the Southeast. By comparison, his opinions would have more weight than yours in front of a jury. Your hair is not as gray. See my point?"

"I see," said Mr. Sterling. "How do you want to handle this?"

"I am going to fax a copy of his report to you," said Cephas. "I want you to read it thoroughly over the weekend. I depose Dr. Thomas on Tuesday of next week. I need you to find something in this report that can be used to chink the armor of Dr. Thomas. Come to think of it, I am going to fax you several of Dr. Thomas' depositions that Bill Buttermore found. Can you sit with me while I depose Dr. Thomas on Tuesday?"

"Sure. I can move things around here," said Mr. Sterling. "What time do you need me in your office Tuesday morning?"

"Seven thirty," said Cephas. "The deposition starts at 9:00. I want to meet with you for about an hour before driving over to Byron Heard's office."

Cephas Hampton sent Mr. Sterling the transcripts of ten depositions. Mr. Sterling began reading them as soon as the first one was received. He read them late into Friday evening, and all day Saturday. In every single deposition, the asphalt mix met the specifications of the states where the mix was placed.

While sitting at his kitchen table having his evening meal, Mr. Sterling had a thought. "Where is Dr. Thomas having the tests performed?"

ooooo

The following Tuesday morning, Allen Sterling arrived at Cephas' office. He sat in the reception area.

Cyndi Carday asked, "Would you like something to drink, Mr. Sterling?"

"No thank you," he said.

Mr. Sterling did not think he had much to tell Cephas. Most of the depositions revealed that Dr. Thomas worked almost exclusively for defendants. The fees he charged for the actual tests were relatively low compared to the amount of testing performed. His personal hourly rate, on the other hand, was the highest Mr. Sterling had ever seen. With a slight smile on his face, he thought to himself that maybe someday, when he grew up, he could command such a fee.

Cephas walked in the reception area and said, "How's it going Mr. Sterling? Any good news?"

"I'm not sure," he said.

"We'll see," said Cephas. "Let's go to the conference room."

Cephas and Mr. Sterling sat down at the conference room table. Mr. Sterling talked about the various issues he had noticed while reading Dr. Thomas' deposition. The conversation eventually focused on the quality of testing, and the personnel performing the testing.

"Are you sure he does his testing at the university?" said Cephas.

"Pretty sure," said Mr. Sterling. "His reports routinely mention the quality testing equipment used at the university. Nowhere do they mention calibration."

"What about the people performing the asphalt testing?" said Cephas.

"This is the really funny part," said Mr. Sterling. "The reports emphasize that all testing is supervised by university personnel. This begs the question, 'Who is the university supervising?'"

"Interesting," said Cephas. "This may lead to something. We need to go."

ooooo

At 8:50 am, Cephas Hampton and Allen Sterling walked into the offices of Byron Heard. The receptionist led them into the conference room where the court reporter, Byron, and Dr. Thaddeus A. Thomas, PhD were already seated.

With a confused look on his face, Byron looked at Cephas and said, "You did not tell me he was coming," referring to Mr. Sterling.

"I know," said Cephas. "There are many technical issues that I need help with. I did not think you'd mind.

Dr. Thomas interjected, in a sarcastic voice, "I could have helped you with anything technical, Mr. Hampton." He shifted his eyes at Mr. Sterling and said, "That is what I am here for."

"I appreciate the gesture, Dr. Thomas," said Cephas. "If it is all the same, I will use Mr. Sterling, if you don't mind."

Dr. Thomas just smiled and thought to himself that this Allen Sterling was a mere child compared to him. Just in his thirties, not even a PhD. This man was going to help an attorney with *my* deposition? His presence offends me. "Whatever you want," said Dr. Thomas to Cephas.

Cephas and Mr. Sterling sat on one side, at the end of the table. Byron and Dr. Thomas sat directly across from them. The court reporter sat at the very end. "I am ready," she said.

Cephas Hampton began with the standard deposition language. "This shall be the deposition of Dr. Thaddeus A. Thomas for the purposes of discovery. It is stipulated that this deposition is taken pursuant to Notice of Taking Deposition and/or agreement of counsel, yet all question as to sufficiency of such Notice or agreement is waived; that all objections, except as to the form of the question, are reserved until the time of trial. Does the witness want to read and sign?"

"I always read and sign," said Dr. Thomas.

"Good," said Cephas. Court reporter, please swear in the witness."

"Do you solemnly swear that the testimony you are about to give will be the truth, the whole truth, and nothing but the truth, so help you God?" said the court reporter.

"I always do," said Dr. Thomas.

Examination by Mr. Hampton

Q   Please state your name and address for the record.

A   My name is Dr. Thaddeus Archibald Thomas, PhD.

Like most depositions, thirty minutes to an hour was spent talking about Dr. Thomas's personal, educational, and professional background.

Q   Let's talk about your work history. Have you ever designed a road or highway?

A   I've designed many job mix designs for numerous DOT's throughout the United States.

Q   That was not what I thought I asked. I will be more specific. Have you ever designed the actual road or highway that was installed by a roadway contractor?

A   No, my work has been in the quality and consistency of the asphalt used in roadway and highway construction.

Q   Have you ever been involved in the actual placement of the asphalt during a roadway construction project?

A   During field trips I would take my classes on when the opportunity arose.

Q   So it would be safe to say that your work involving the asphalt in a roadway or highway project would be theoretical with regard to the asphalt pavement mix design?

Dr. Thomas grew angry at this line of questioning. Cephas Hampton had hoped for such a reaction.

A   My work is beyond theoretical. The asphalt mixes I design are used by DOT's throughout the United States.

Q   Very good. These asphalt mix designs you produce – what equipment do you use to create these asphalt mix designs?

A   I use the equipment at our university materials laboratory.

Q   Do you run the equipment yourself, or do you use others?

A   As part of their education, undergraduate and graduate students are given the opportunity to use this equipment – under my supervision, of course.

Q   Of course. What kind of equipment is used for asphalt mix design?

A   We have equipment to determine the size and amounts of sand and rock in the asphalt mix. There is equipment to determine the strength of the asphalt mix. There is equipment to heat and cool the asphalt mix to run specific tests required by a DOT.

Q   Do you use scales to weigh the asphalt mix?

A   Oh, definitely. Weight scales are used at almost every step of the asphalt testing.

Q   How old are the equipment and weight scales you use at your materials laboratory?

A   They are between ten and fifteen years old.

Q   Who maintains these items?

A   I do, or I should say, my students do.

Q   Are the equipment and weight scales you use for the asphalt mix design the same that you used to evaluate the asphalt placed by Bishop Construction?

A   Yes.

At about that moment, Byron sensed a problem, but he was not sure what it was.

Q   And it is your opinion that the asphalt placed by Bishop Construction was within all the parameters of the SCDOT road specification?

A   It was in every way.

For the remainder of the deposition, Cephas went back and forth with questions about Dr. Thomas' work history and educational background. As expected, his answers did not change. Byron thought this tactic very strange. "Why is Cephas not hammering Dr. Thomas on his opinions? Why were they only touched on once?

ooooo

In the weeks that followed Dr. Thomas' deposition, the negotiations were almost non-stop. Cephas started the negotiations with a demand of policy limits at $500,000. Byron countered with $200,000. After four weeks of negotiations, Byron's number was $250,000. This case was going to trial.

15 - THE TRIAL

The judge chosen to preside over this trial was Judge Joseph C. Aiken. Judge Aiken was known throughout Beaufort County as a fair man. He had started his legal career working as a defense attorney. As an associate attorney for a large firm for fifteen years, he worked cases for many insurance companies. For a change of pace, he took a position with a plaintiff's firm in Beaufort County. He held that position for ten years when an opportunity arose to be elected as a judge in Beaufort County. Judge Aiken was very popular with both the defense and plaintiff's attorneys in the area because of the relationships he had made with them throughout the years. He won the election by an overwhelming majority of votes.

Judge Aiken set the trial start date for Monday, November 9, 1992. Jury selection would commence first thing that morning, and the jury would be seated by the end of business that day. All parties agreed that every consideration would be given to Dr. Christine Jesup with regard to her medical needs and personal comforts.

ooooo

On the Friday before jury selection, all doctors, lawyers, witnesses and all of their support personnel, for both plaintiff and defense, descended onto Beaufort. The only motel large enough and available to support these two groups was the Patriot Motel, just outside Beaufort. The Patriot Motel's office was a two-story structure with the office on the bottom level, and the owner's living quarters on the upper level. On each side of the two-story structure was a wing of ten rooms. To look at the motel from above one would think he was looking at a delta winged military bomber. That each of the rooms had its own bathroom and telephone was thought of as a significant improvement to the other motels in that part of Beaufort. The people representing the plaintiffs were located in the left wing. Those representing the defense were in the right wing.

ooooo

Twelve jury members were selected from the jury pool of fifty people who showed up the following Monday at the Beaufort County Courthouse as directed by the Clerk of the Court. Cephas Hampton and Byron Heard were each given six strikes to remove a person from jury consideration. The final jury members had not been selected by lunch, but the remaining jury members were selected by four o'clock. All of the jury members were longtime residents of Beaufort County. They ranged in age from twenty five to fifty-five. There were seven females and five males. Ten were white, and two were black. But the most significant statistic – one that gave Cephas comfort and Byron discomfort – was that seven of the jury members were parents or grandparents of babies delivered by Dr. Christine Jesup. The other five jury members were friends of parents or grandparents of babies delivered by Dr. Jesup.

"Your Honor," said Byron to Judge Aiken in the judge's office, "this is not an impartial jury for my client. I would like to reinstate my motion for a change in venue. Orangeburg County is a more than fair location for this trial to take place."

"Judge Aiken," said Cephas, "as I have explained to Mr. Heard repeatedly, Dr. Jesup is a quadriplegic. She cannot move anything below her neck. Her medical requirements are quite extensive. They require twenty-four hour, seven day a week care from trained people. To require her to relocate to Orangeburg County for this trial would be a severe personal and financial hardship, if not downright cruel. I ask that the trial remain in Beaufort County."

When both men finished, Judge Aiken looked down at the doctor's report Cephas had given him. The report outlined the daily hour-by-hour routine of Dr. Jesup. According to the report, to relocate Dr. Jesup would require not only her to move, but also three medical personnel and two private care givers.

"Gentlemen," said Judge Aiken, "I understand Mr. Heard's concern about the jury. A snapshot of this jury could give a person pause regarding just how impartial they could be. But, as a defense and plaintiff's attorney in the county for many years, I have found that the people of Beaufort

County want to be fair. They know their role. They will hear the evidence and decide accordingly. Be that as it may, the august role of our jury is secondary to the needs of Dr. Jesup. From what I have read, she cannot move from one room to the other without assistance. With that said, I maintain my decision to keep the trial in Beaufort County."

"Thank you, Your Honor," said Cephas.

"Your Honor," said Byron, "I respectfully establish notice that should a jury verdict not go my client's way, I will be appealing the verdict to the State Supreme Court based on this decision, and others that may occur during trial."

"That is your right," said Judge Aiken.

"Thank you, Your Honor," said Byron.

"That will be all, gentlemen," said the judge as both men turned and walked out of his office.

Out in the corridor, Cephas turned to Byron and said, "Five hundred thousand is a fair number and you know it, Byron. Are you even thinking about it?"

"Cephas," said Byron, "all I need is one jury member to vote my way. I know it, you know it, and most importantly, my client knows it. Unless you get off your five hundred thousand dollar high horse and get reasonable, your client will get nothing. My offer stands at $250,000."

Cephas and Byron stood motionless in the center of the corridor with people walking past them on all sides. Several passersby found it odd to see two men standing so motionless and looking directly at each other. Each was carrying a briefcase in his right hand. Each looked sternly and directly into the eyes of the other. Cephas thought to himself, "I've known this man for over twenty years. When did he turn into such an ass?"

"Please take the offer, Cephas," thought Byron, doing his best not to telegraph his fear.

"See you at nine am sharp, my friend," said Cephas as he turned and walks away.

ooooo

At 8:45 am on Tuesday, November 10, Dr. Christine Dee Jesup entered the courtroom of Judge Joseph C. Aiken. The double doors were opened by deputies. The special wheelchair Dr. Bishop occupied was being pushed by Jack Jesup, her father. The wheelchair was specially designed to hold up her head, and had a device to keep her legs against the chair. As she traveled down the center aisle, she looked to her right and saw Dr. Honeycutt sitting just behind the plaintiff's table. He sent a friendly smile to her. She managed a smile back.

Already at the plaintiff's table was Cephas Hampton. He stood up and went over to the double swinging gates at the rail which separated the gallery from the actual court area. As he held them open, Dr. Jesup was rolled over to the end of the table farthest from the gates. Jack Jesup took the seat next to his daughter. Cephas took the seat closest to the gates.

At the defendant's table across from the gates sat attorney Byron Heard and his client, Nathan Bishop. Neither one acknowledged the entrance of Dr. Jesup. As instructed, Nathan sat motionless, looking forward, with his hands crossed on the table; just like Byron's.

In the first row, right behind the defendant's table, sat Shirley Stone of Fidelis Mutual. She could not keep herself from looking at Dr. Jesup and thinking, "Oh my Lord, I did not know they taught theatrics this far south."

ooooo

"All rise," said the bailiff, Sheriff's Deputy Floyd Tarpley, at 9:01 am. "Court is now in session. The Honorable Judge Joseph C. Aiken presiding."

Judge Aiken looked out over the gallery and said, "You may be seated."

The noise of people sitting down caught his attention. The courtroom was almost full. Judge Aiken thought to himself, "Normally it's the criminal court cases that bring out the people."

Judge Aiken picked up a manila file and opens it and begins to read,

"This is the matter of Christine Dee Jesup v. Bishop Construction Company." Without looking up, he said, "Are both parties present?"

"Yes, Your Honor," said Cephas and Byron.

"Good," said Judge Aiken, taking a slight pause to read more of the file.

He looked up at both Cephas and Byron and asked, "Are you ready for your opening statements, gentlemen?"

"Yes, Your Honor," said Cephas and Byron.

"Mr. Hampton, you may begin."

Cephas , more so than most attorneys, understood the power of the presentation. To be a good trial attorney was not only to have knowledge of the law, but also to have proper packaging. One had to look like an attorney. The seersucker suit accomplished this. Besides, who better to emulate than Gregory Peck as Atticus Finch in "To Kill a Mockingbird?"

Cephas stood up, walked around to the front of his table and began his opening statement:

"Ladies and gentlemen of the jury, each one of you is here today as a trier of fact. As such, you will hear and see evidence regarding the tragedy that caused Dr. Christine Jesup to become a quadriplegic. That's right. She cannot move her body from the neck down. Dr. Jesup had a blossoming career as a doctor at Beaufort Memorial. She was, and still is, loved by those in the community she served."

Cephas turned his attention to the floor just in front of his feet while pausing his opening statement for a few seconds. He raised his head slowly.

" You will hear and see evidence that Old Sheldon Church Road was being overlaid with two additional inches of asphalt pavement. You will hear and see evidence that Dr. Jesup was attending to her secured pregnant patient in an ambulance headed for Beaufort Memorial. You will hear and see evidence that the ambulance abruptly turned to the right side of the road because of a deer. The ambulance tried to re-enter the road, but was denied easy access because of an eight-inch difference between the shoulder and the roadway surface. This was compounded by an apparent defect in the asphalt mix that caused it not to hold together. When the ambulance finally got onto the road, the steering to the left was so severe that as it was about to hit an oncoming vehicle, the ambulance driver turned right to miss the vehicle, and turned the ambulance on its side. The ambulance crashed into an oak tree. As a result, Dr. Jesup broke her neck. It is our contention that the asphalt mix produced by Bishop Construction was made defective in order to save money. It is our contention that no warnings were given about the depth of the shoulder, and that no signage was present to warn the ambulance driver of the recent roadway construction work – again to save money. It is our contention that Bishop Construction was responsible for warning the public about the construction work and shoulder. It is our contention that Bishop Construction Company was responsible for this incident. You will hear and see evidence from the defense that the asphalt was fine, and that the absence of warnings and signage was proper."

Cephas took a few steps toward the jury box.

"I ask each of you, an honorable trier of fact, to hear and see the truth of all this evidence and to find some modicum of relief for Dr. Christine Jesup. Thank you."

Cephas walked back to the plaintiffs table and took his seat.

"Byron, you may begin."
"Thank you, Your Honor," said Byron.

Byron stood up, but did not come from behind his table. He looked toward the jury.

With a loud, baritone voice, he said, "That Christine Jesup is a quadriplegic is a tragedy. Of that, there is no doubt. And yes, some of what Mr. Hampton said is true. Each and every one of you is a trier of the facts in the case. And yes, you will hear and see much evidence about my client's contractual obligation to install the asphalt pavement overlay."

Byron stepped to his right from behind the defense table, while never taking his eyes off the jury.

Moving toward the jury with one step per sentence, he said, "But Mr. Hampton has one problem. He has to prove his case. He has to show evidence that the asphalt pavement was bad. He has to show evidence that these warnings he speaks of were required even though the contract was mute on the subject." Byron stopped about six feet from the jury rail.

"Mr. Hampton will try and prove his case with the use of an expert witness with supposed credentials in roadway construction and materials. His experts name is Georgia Tech *assistant* professor, *Mister* Allen Peter Sterling. Our expert is *Doctor*, and tenured professor, Thaddeus A. Thomas of the University of Alabama. We look forward to the comparison. Thank you."

Byron turned, walked back to the table, and took his seat.

"Mr. Hampton, are you ready with your direct examination?" said Judge Aiken
"Yes sir, Your Honor. I would like to begin by calling Beatrice Pitts to the stand."

Cephas Hampton began his case by calling the EMT personnel that had been accompanying Dr. Jesup to the hospital at the time of the accident. After Ms. Pitts testified, Gerald Toombs took the stand. Both established that what they were doing at the time of the incident was routine. Both testified that it was normal for a doctor to unbuckle in order to take care of a patient. During cross examination, Byron repeatedly asked Betty Pitts if leaving the road was the smartest thing to do. She was repeatedly consistent in her answer that it was either leave the road, or hit the deer. Besides, she had had cause to leave paved roads numerous times because of deer and other objects. Each other time, she had been able to smoothly transition from the shoulder to the road.

After lunch, Cephas called Allen Peter Sterling, PE, to the stand. Mr. Sterling took the seat in the witness box.

"Please state your name for the jury, Mr. Sterling," said Cephas.

"My name is Allen Peter Sterling."

"Thank you. Please tell us your educational and professional background," said Cephas.

For the next ten minutes, Mr. Sterling told the jury his educational background and his work history.

"Thank you, Mr. Sterling. Your Honor, if there are no objections, I respectfully request that you find Mr. Sterling a qualified expert witness at this time."

Byron quickly stood up and said, "Your Honor, I object to this witness being considered an expert. While I will yield to the fact that he is a licensed engineer in Georgia, he is not licensed in South Carolina to practice engineering. In addition, I submit that his experience and current status as an assistant professor makes him more qualified to be a technician in road design and construction, rather than an engineer in South Carolina."

Cephas looked directly at the judge and said, "My esteemed colleague would have us conveniently forget Mr. Sterling's peer-reviewed papers, his status as a sought-after lecturer, his work as an actual roadway designer and inspector. Shall I go on, Your Honor?

"That's enough, gentlemen. With regard to Mr. Sterling's status as an expert, his education and experience more than qualify him as an expert in this court. With regard to Mr. Sterling's licensure status?" Judge Aiken took a moment to think about the situation.

Judge Aiken said, "We have a licensing board in the state of South Carolina that determines whether or not to give a license to individuals in order for them to practice engineering in our state. This licensing board is established by our governor. The governor is the executive branch of our state government. I am a member of the judicial branch. I know of no law from the legislative branch regarding out-of-state licensed engineers. As we all know, or should know, from the separation of powers doctrine of our federal and state constitutions, each branch of government is independent of the other. With that said, I am under no obligation to require engineering licensure as a condition of being an expert witness just because the subject expert is licensed in another state. The jury may use the fact that Mr. Sterling is not licensed in South Carolina to determine the weight of Mr. Sterling's testimony. As for me, I find Mr. Sterling more than qualified."

"Thank you, Your Honor, "said Cephas. "Mr. Sterling, please allow the court reporter to swear you in."

After Mr. Sterling was sworn in, Cephas began his questioning. Mr. Sterling explained the need for warning signage, and how there had been inadequate signage at each end of the work zone. He went on to explain the danger caused by the eight-inch drop-off from the roadway to the shoulder, and how that danger was not conveyed to the public. He told how the asphalt mix was defective, and how this dust-to-asphalt ratio defect contributed to the ambulance not being able to re-mount the roadway.

At about 3:00 pm, Cephas Hampton finished his questioning of Mr. Sterling.

"Byron, do you wish to cross-examine the witness?" said Judge Aiken.

"Very much so, Your Honor," said Byron.

"You may proceed," said Judge Aiken.

"Mr. Sterling, where does it say specifically and clearly in the roadway specifications that Bishop Construction was responsible for correcting the shoulder drop-off you have been opining about?"

"As I testified earlier," said Mr. Sterling, "the Red Book stated, and I quote, the contractor will be required without direct compensation to maintain in good condition the entire section or sections of highway within the limits of the contract, from the time he first begins work until all work has been completed and accepted."

"So you admit there is nothing specific and clear in the roadway specifications?" said Byron.

"I do *not* admit that," said Mr. Sterling. "It is my opinion that Bishop Construction did not maintain the road in good condition. As a result, the eight inch drop-off was one of the proximate causes of this accident that caused Dr. Jesup to become a quadriplegic."

"We know your opinions as a plaintiff's expert, Mr. Sterling, "said Byron. "What I am having a problem with is that contracts are supposed to be clear and specific. You are not helping in that regard."

"Objection, You Honor," said Cephas. "Mr. Heard is just being argumentative with Mr. Sterling. This does not seem necessary."

"Objection sustained, "said Judge Aiken. "Mr. Heard, your commentary is not appropriate at this time. Please ask your questions and move on."

"Yes, Your Honor," said Byron. "Mr. Sterling, you stated earlier in your examination by Mr. Hampton that you have a problem with the asphalt mix, specifically the dust-to-asphalt ratio. It that correct?"

"Yes, sir," he said.

"That it was this dust-to-asphalt ratio that contributed to this accident, is that correct?" said Byron.

"Yes," said Mr. Sterling waiting for what he was sure was about to come.

"Good," said Byron. He turned and walked toward the defense table. He picked up a copy of Mr. Sterling's deposition and walked over to the rail in front of him.

"Mr. Sterling," said Byron, "this is a copy of your deposition that you gave several months ago. Do you agree that this is your deposition?"

"It appears to be," said Mr. Sterling, after thumbing through the pages.

"Good," said Byron. "Do you remember me asking you about the different parts of an asphalt specification?"

"I do," said Mr. Sterling.

"In fact," said Byron, "you answered that there were many parts of an asphalt specification, and that each had to be correct or the mix was defective. You likened it to baking a cake, if my memory serves me. Do you remember comparing an asphalt mix to *baked goods*, Mr. Sterling?

"You asked me why the dust-to-asphalt ratio was so important compared to the other aspects of an asphalt mix," said Mr. Sterling. "As someone who has to cook for himself, I know that if you mess up one thing in a cake mix, the whole thing could be ruined. The analogy fits."

Byron leaned in toward Mr. Sterling and asked, "The dust-to-asphalt ratio was the *only* thing you found wrong with the asphalt mix, is that correct?

"Correct," said Mr. Sterling.

"You know Dr. Thomas, don't you?" said Byron.

"We met at his deposition for this case," said Mr. Sterling. "I knew about him before we met through shared colleagues."

"Do you have anything critical to say about Dr. Thomas, either personally or professionally, outside this case," said Byron.

"No," said Mr. Sterling

"So, it is my understanding that you are critical of the asphalt mix produced by Bishop Construction Company, and that Dr. Thomas has found nothing to be critical of in the asphalt mix, correct?"

"You understand correctly," said Mr. Sterling.

"Before I finish with you, I have one more question," said Byron. "Dr. Thomas is a tenured professor at the University of Alabama, correct?"

"That is correct," said Mr. Sterling.

"And you are *not* a tenured professor, correct?" said Byron.

"Not yet," said Mr. Sterling.

"Good enough. That is all I need of this witness, Your Honor," said Byron.

"It is almost five o'clock," said Judge Aiken. "We shall reconvene at nine o'clock tomorrow morning. Court is adjourned."

With that, Bailiff Floyd Tarpley said, "All rise." After everyone stood up that could stand up, Judge Aiken retired to his chambers. The crowd in the gallery ambled out into the lobby while talking about the day's activities.

Cephas looked toward Byron and said, "It was a good day for you, Byron. Things will not be so good for you tomorrow, my friend. Let's settle this for five million and save ourselves future aggravation."

"Cephas," said Byron, "the cost of today's settlement will be $300,000 and not a penny more."

Christine Jesup and her father were still sitting at the end of the plaintiff's table, and heard the conversation between Cephas and Byron. As Byron finished his sentence with "not a penny more," he accidently looked away from Cephas and directly at Christine. Her jaw was fixed, and the skin at her jaw was bunched up because of the head brace, which did not allow her to show emotion with her mouth. However, her eyes were free to move. Byron saw sadness in Christine's eyes. Byron then turned to look at Shirley Stone. By contrast, her eyes were full of satisfaction from the day's events.

ooooo

At 9:00 am, Wednesday, November 11, all parties were in their place. Floyd Tarpley stood and said, "All rise. Court is now in session. The Honorable Judge Joseph C. Aiken presiding."

Judge Aiken walked to his chair, took his seat, looked out over the gallery and said, "Thank you. You may be seated. Mr. Hampton, do you have any more witnesses to call?"

"Only one, Your Honor. I wish to call Dr. Christine Dee Jesup to the stand."

"Very well," said Judge Aiken. "Please place Dr. Jesup in front of the witness box. Will that suffice, Mr. Hampton?"

"Yes, sir," said Cephas.

Cephas maneuvered Dr. Jesup's wheelchair from the plaintiff's table to in front of the witness box. He angled Dr. Jesup slightly toward the jury so that they could see her face.

Stepping in front of Dr. Jesup, Cephas turned toward Judge Aiken and said, "Your Honor, I respectively request that you ask the jury, the gallery, and all those present, with the exception of Mr. Heard and yourself, to remain silent and still during the questioning of Dr. Jesup. As we all know, Dr. Jesup is paralyzed from the neck down. Fortunately, her voice still works; although at a reduced volume. I would like the jury to hear her answers to my, and Mr. Heard's, questions."

Judge Aiken looked into the gallery and said, "Please, everyone. Please remain silent and very still while Dr. Jesup is being questioned. No whispers, opening of candy wrappers, or anything else will be tolerated while she is being questioned."

"Thank you, Your Honor," said Cephas Hampton. He turned toward the court reporter and asked her to swear in Dr. Jesup.

"Do you solemnly swear to tell the truth, the whole truth, so help you God?" said the court reporter.

"I do," said Christine Jesup.

Cephas said, "Good morning, Dr. Jesup."

"Good morning, Mr. Hampton," said Christine.

"Dr. Jesup, please tell us your full name and date of birth," said Cephas.

For the next thirty minutes to an hour, Cephas Hampton asked Christine about her upbringing in Beaufort County. She told how she went to medical school at the encouragement of Dr. Maurice Honeycutt, and she came back to Beaufort to practice medicine at Beaufort Memorial Hospital.

"Thank you, Dr. Jesup," said Cephas. "Now, we have heard much testimony about the day you were injured. I am not going to ask you about that. What I am going to ask about are your days since the crash. Specifically, would you please tell us about a normal day in the life of Dr. Christine Jesup."

"May I have a drink of water?" said Christine.
"Do you need to take a break?" asked Cephas.
"No. I just need a little water for my throat. I would like to finish talking with you this morning, if I could," she said.
"Of course," said Cephas.

Dr. Jesup's father stood up, poured a glass of water from the pitcher on the table, and walked it over to his daughter. He poured water into the open lips. She coughed a bit, causing some of the water to spill onto her clothing.

"I'm sorry," said Dr. Jesup.

Cephas took out his handkerchief and dabbed it on the water stains.

"No problem," he said.
"Where do I start?" said Christine.
"Let's start with when you wake up. Let's start there," said Cephas.
"Well," she said, "like most people, right when I get up, I have to use the bathroom."

For the next hour, Dr. Christine Jesup described, in detail, what was necessary for her to live what was a normal day for her. As a quadriplegic, one, if not two, nurses or aides, were needed to move her, and to remove her feces and urine from her genital area. All her meals were made for her, and given to her, by someone. Because she could not move, she had to be constantly checked for bed sores and other skin problems. Because she still had her mind, she was very depressed. Her daily routine included the taking of many antidepressant and anti-anxiety medications. She slept constantly during the day, and often took sleeping pills at night. While the doctors said that she might regain some of her movement, it would likely takes years, if not decades, of physical and occupational therapy just to be able to stand up with a walker. And the last thing she said to the court: "I miss being a doctor. I miss delivering babies. And most of all, I miss just being able to live like I used to."

When Christine quit talking, the courtroom was silent. Every single juror was looking at her. Christine's head was being held up by braces so that only her face was visible. And on that face, the jury could see a tear on her cheek.

Behind Byron Heard sat Shirley Stone of Fidelis Mutual. Many on the jury took notice of her because she had been sitting in the same spot for the past two days, and was constantly tapping on Byron's shoulder and whispering in his ear. At times, they almost appeared to be arguing. At this particular moment, while looking at Dr. Jesup, she was smiling and slowly shaking her head to the left and right; as if in disbelief. Many on the jury noticed.

"Thank you, Christine," said Cephas. He turned toward Byron and said, "Your witness."

Byron had known from the beginning what he was going to do at this moment. To ask Dr. Jesup any questions would only make him look like a bully. To just appear like he was hurting her would make it look like he was stepping on a kitten.

"No questions," he said.

Judge Aiken said, "It is almost eleven. Court will be in recess until one o'clock.

"All rise," said Floyd Tarpley. Judge Aiken stood up and walked to his chambers.

ooooo

At one o'clock sharp Floyd Tarpley stood up and said to the people in the courtroom, "All rise, court is now in session."

Judge Aiken took his seat, looked over to Byron and said, "Are you ready, Mr. Heard?"

"Yes, Your Honor," said Byron.

"You may call your first witness," said the judge.

"I call Dr. Thaddeus A. Thomas," said Byron.

Dr. Thomas stood up from his gallery seat behind the defense table, and walked toward the witness stand without any emotion on his face.

"Madam court reporter, please swear in the witness," said Byron.

"Please raise your right hand. Do you solemnly swear to tell the truth, the whole truth and nothing but the truth, so help you God?" said the court reporter.

"Of course," said Dr. Thomas.

For thirty minutes, Dr. Thomas told the jury about his educational and professional background. Explaining his professional background took the longest, due to the number of assignments he had taken from multiple state transportation departments, and from his legal work for those same clients.

After Dr. Thomas answered the last question, Byron said, "Your Honor, I respectively request that you deem Dr. Thomas qualified as an expert witness."

At that moment, Cephas stood up and said, "Your Honor, I would like an opportunity to question Dr. Thomas before he is deemed qualified."

"Go ahead," said Judge Aiken.

"Thank you, Your Honor," said Cephas. "Dr. Thomas, you performed many asphalt tests, and generated many results that you base your opinion on here today, correct?"

"That is correct," said Dr. Thomas.

"Who actually performed the tests?" said Cephas.

"As I stated in my deposition, I supervised the undergraduate and graduate students who were in my materials testing classes at the time," said Dr. Thomas.

"So, is it safe to say that these people who were performing the tests were not certified or trained by any national organization, such as the Asphalt Institute, on how to perform these tests, correct? You did know that the Asphalt Institute certifies people to perform asphalt testing, didn't you, Dr. Thomas?"

"Yes, I know what the Asphalt Institute does. And no, my students did not need any certification. They had me to supervise," said Dr. Thomas.

It was at this moment that both Dr. Thomas and Byron Heard felt a pain their stomachs. Many in the jury had not been sure if Dr. Thomas was arrogant. That last answer removed any doubt.

"No certification from the Asphalt Institute," said Cephas as he looked down and walked away from Dr. Thomas. He stopped, turned around, and asked Dr. Thomas, "The weight measuring scales and other devices you used for the testing; were they certified or calibrated by any national organization like, say, the National Institute of Standards and Technology, the NIST? You have heard of the NIST, haven't you, Dr. Thomas?"

"Yes, I have heard of the NIST. And no, they were not looked at by them," said Dr. Thomas with an irritated tone and with an irritated look on his face. "They were routinely maintained and cleaned by me and my students."

"How old were these scales, Dr. Thomas?" said Cephas.

"Fifteen years old," said Dr. Thomas.

"So," said Cephas as he walked toward the witness stand and stopped at the rail, "you use uncertified students to perform tests using un-calibrated equipment. Why are we to believe that these tests results are reliable?"

"Because I said so," said Dr. Thomas.

Cephas' eyes were now wide open with his mouth the same way. He could not believe the amount of hubris sitting before him.

Stepping backward he looked towards the judge and said, "Your Honor, I respectfully request that Dr. Thomas *not* be allowed to testify as an expert witness because every single one of his opinions are based on work performed by uncertified and unqualified students who performed their work on unreliable equipment that has never been calibrated."

All eyes turned toward Judge Aiken. He sat there for a moment thinking about what had just been said.

Realizing what could happen, Byron jumped up from his seat and said, "Side bar, Your Honor." Judge Aiken motioned for each attorney to approach the bench.

"Your Honor," said Byron, "Dr. Thomas is a tenured professor, a sought-after engineer and has provided expert witness testimony in numerous cases all over the United States. He should be found more than qualified as an expert witness."

"Your Honor," said Cephas, "has anyone ever thoroughly questioned Dr. Thomas about his methods of asphalt testing? The qualifications of the people doing the testing? The use of proper equipment? Your Honor, these are important issues that I respectfully request Dr. Thomas explain to you before you make a decision."

"Gentlemen, please take your seats," said Judge Aiken.

After Cephas and Byron took their seats, Judge Aiken said, "Ladies and gentlemen of the jury, the lawyers and I have a legal question that must be addressed. I am going to adjourn court for today so that I can meet with the lawyers and discuss this issue. It is two o'clock. I want Mr. Heard, Mr. Hampton, and Dr. Thomas to be in my chambers at 2:30. Jurors, I will see you tomorrow morning at nine o'clock. Court is adjourned."

"All rise," said Floyd Tarpley. Judge Aiken walked to his chambers while the gallery emptied.

Byron Heard walked up to the witness stand where Dr. Thomas was still sitting. He turned toward the gallery and made sure no one was still there.

He turned towards Dr. Thomas and said, "Because you said so? What the hell was that all about?"

"My opinions have *never* been questioned, least of all my testing methods," said Dr. Thomas. "Who does this Cephas Hampton think he is?"

"I'll tell you who he is," said Byron. "He is a lawyer that has the judge thinking. You get on the phone and have your people fax over to me anything that shows the maintenance of the equipment."

"There is nothing," said Dr. Thomas. "Maintenance is something we do as part of the class. No records are kept."

"Dr. Thomas," said Byron, "at 2:30 you better be ready to put on the charm and professionalism. Do you understand what could happen?"

"Mr. Heard," said Dr. Thomas, "I did not come all the way out here just to have some country judge tell me whether my opinions are good or not. I have never lost a case. My opinions have always been accepted. This will not be the first."

"You'd better be right, Dr. Thomas," said Byron. "Otherwise, we are going to have a problem."

ooooo

At 2:30, Cephas Hampton, Byron Heard, and Dr. Thaddeus Thomas were sitting in the judge's anteroom, just outside his chambers. A clerk walked in and said to the group, "The judge will see you now." They stood up and walked into the judge's chambers, where a sheriff's deputy was holding the door open. Judge Aiken was already sitting behind his desk, and the court reporter was sitting to the side of the judge's desk.

"Gentlemen, please be seated," said Judge Aiken.

Byron and Cephas both said, "Thank you, Your Honor." Dr. Thomas said nothing as he sat down. Judge Aiken noticed. He nodded to the court reporter to begin.

"Gentlemen," said Judge Aiken, "let's begin this way. Mr. Hampton, you made some serious allegations regarding Dr. Thomas' people and the equipment they used. Tell me why the testing results that your expert used are any better."

"Gladly, Your Honor," said Cephas. "Allen Sterling, my expert in this matter, procured the services of Harry Corn of PST Laboratories once the asphalt samples were taken from Old Sheldon Church Road. PST is a well-known laboratory that performs testing for numerous state DOT's throughout the southeastern United States."

Cephas reached into his briefcase and pulled out a folder.

"Your Honor," said Cephas, "I offer to the court copies of all the certifications of all personnel who performed the tests on the asphalt taken by Allen Sterling. These certifications show that they have the competency and training required by the Asphalt Institute to perform asphalt testing. In addition, Your Honor, I offer the court copies of all the calibration certifications of all the equipment at PST used for the asphalt testing required by Mr. Sterling. Note that the calibration of this equipment was performed yearly, and the calibration meets the standards of the National Institute of Standards and Testing, the NIST. You asked why the testing results used by Mr. Sterling are better. They are better because they are reliable, and can be traced back to national standards."

Judge Aiken had been sitting back in his leather chair, legs crossed, and hands folded in his lap the whole time Cephas was speaking.

He looked towards Byron Heard and said, "What do you have that shows that the test results relied upon by your expert are reliable, Mr. Heard?"

"Your Honor, Dr. Thomas is an esteemed, tenured professor at one of the largest universities, with one of the largest material testing labs, in the Southeast. His credentials, his methods, have never been questioned until today. He has performed thousands of different asphalt tests for countless clients. That has to count for something." Byron thought to himself that Dr. Thomas' celebrity was the only thread of hope to salvage this situation.

Judge Aiken looked towards Dr. Thomas and said, "Dr. Thomas, you receive fees for the testing you, or should I say your students, perform for private clients like Byron and the various state DOT's, correct?"

"Yes," said Dr. Thomas.

"I will limit the timeframe of my question to the past fifteen years because that is the age of your equipment," said Judge Aiken. "Dr. Thomas, in the past fifteen years, have you ever had one of your students, or the methods by which you teach your students, evaluated by the Asphalt

Institute with regard to the procedures used for asphalt testing?"

"No," said Dr. Thomas. "It was not necessary because they were guided by me, and..."

"It was a 'yes' or 'no' question, Dr. Thomas," said Judge Aiken. "If I want commentary, I will ask for it."

Dr. Thomas was not accustomed to being spoken to that way. His face and body language reeked of contempt for this whole situation.

"One last question, Dr. Thomas," said Judge Aiken. "In the past fifteen years, has any of the equipment you, or your students used, in the performance of asphalt testing ever been calibrated to national standards?"

"No," said Dr. Thomas. "May I explain that..."

"No, you may not explain," said Judge Aiken. "Your last response in court explains it all: 'Because I said so'. Dr. Thomas, you are a learned man. Are you familiar with the Latin phrase *Ipse Dixit?*"

"No," said Dr. Thomas.

"I am surprised," said Judge Aiken. "It describes you perfectly. It roughly means that a statement or evidence is valid, 'because I said so.' Let's not waste any more time. It is my judgment that the opinions generated by Dr. Thomas regarding the quality of the asphalt produced by Bishop Construction will not be heard by the jury. It is my judgment that the test results produced by Dr. Thomas are unreliable, thus the opinions generated from those test results are unreliable."

At that moment, Dr. Thomas stood up and said loudly, "*Who* are *you* to judge me, or *anything* I do?"

The sheriff's deputy instinctively drew his baton and walked toward Dr. Thomas. He started to raise the baton.

Judge Aiken held his hand up toward the deputy and said, "Stop! That won't be necessary."

"Mr. Heard," said Judge Aiken, "tell your expert to set his butt down right now or I will ask this deputy to jail him for ten days for contempt of court – the hard way. Do you both understand?"

Byron stood up, cupped Dr. Thomas's arm with both hands and said, "Dr. Thomas, we still need you. If you go to jail, our case is sunk. Please sit down or the judge will send you to jail."

Dr. Thomas slowly sat down. He only sat on the edge of the chair with his body leaning toward Judge Aiken.

"Good," said Judge Aiken with a smile on his face. "we now have order. Mr. Heard, I will allow you to use the testimony of Dr. Thomas with regard to the construction site signage. He will not be allowed to opine on the quality of the asphalt."

Byron said, "But Your Honor, we need time to retest and..."

"Mr. Heard," said Judge Aiken, "you had your chance. I will not allow you to waste the time of this court. I will see you tomorrow morning in court, where you will continue with your defense. This meeting is adjourned."

Cephas was the first to stand up, say, "Thank you, Your Honor," and walked toward the door to exit the judge's chambers. He was ecstatically happy. He could not believe what had just happened. He had gotten the opinions of a tenured professor kicked off a case. He had almost seen that professor get a beating and go to jail. He thought, "You can only be so lucky," with a grin on his face.

Byron stood up and waited for Dr. Thomas to stand. With the watchful eye of a deputy only a few feet away, Dr. Thomas averted his stare from Judge Aiken to the law books behind the judge. He stood up, turned away from Byron, and walked out without saying a word.

Byron turned toward Judge Aiken and said, "Thank you, sir. See you tomorrow."

As Byron exited the door from the anteroom to the courthouse hallway, he was met by Cephas, who was sitting on a wooden bench on the other side of the hallway.

"Byron, can we talk for a few minutes?" said Cephas.

"Why, so you can gloat?" said Byron.

"No," said Cephas, "We need to talk settlement."

Byron sat down on the other end of the bench.

"Are you ready to accept $300,000?" said Byron, attempting to be serious.

Cephas sat there for a few seconds. He could not believe what Byron had just said.

"Were you in the same room with me just a few minutes ago?" said Cephas. "Did you hear the same things I just heard in the judge's chambers? Did you hear Judge Aiken kick out the opinions of your expert witness?"

"Cephas, the number is $300,000," said Byron. "Nothing more."

"Byron, I do not know what you are thinking, but you have got to see things as they are, you…"

"Cephas," said Byron, "don't lecture me. I know the lay of the land as good as anyone. I need only one juror to see things my way – only one. I know it. You know it. And most importantly, my client knows it. That is how things are."

"Byron," said Cephas, "you have until tonight to work this out with your client. We want the policy limits. We will accept nothing less at this time. And remember, if this goes to the jury, the price of cheese will go up."

Byron attempted a slight grin as he stood up and walked away from Cephas, and toward the front entrance of the courthouse. He was furious. This kind of thing had never happened to him before.

Waiting at the bottom of the front steps was Dr. Thomas.

As Byron was walking down the courthouse steps, he said, "Dr. Thomas, do you like teaching?"

"Of course I do," said Dr. Thomas with a tone of righteous indignation.

"Good," said Byron. "Because after today, it is doubtful that you will ever be doing anything else."

Byron reached the bottom of the courthouse steps and said, "Dr. Thomas, you will testify tomorrow morning on how the cones, barrels, and other safety signage were not needed where the ambulance turned over."

"I will not," said Dr. Thomas. "I am through with this case. I am going home."

"Dr. Thomas," said Byron, "you will testify the way I tell you to testify, and you will do it with a smile on your face. And in exchange, I will consider not filing a lawsuit against you for professional incompetence. In addition, I will consider not making you refund the tens of thousands of dollars I have paid you for this and other cases you have worked with me before. Are we in agreement?"

Dr. Thomas took a moment to consider his situation. He thought to himself, "So, this is what humble pie tastes like."

"What do you want me to say?" said Dr. Thomas.
"Good," said Byron. "We will talk tonight at the hotel after dinner."

ooooo

After court that day, Cephas asked Christine Jesup and her father to meet him at his motel room. Mr. Sterling was allowed to sit in and listen. Cyndi Carday was also present to help Cephas with anything else that was needed.

"They are really playing hardball," said Cephas to the group. "I told them that they had until tonight to work this out. I will send Cyndi over in a few minutes with a piece of paper with a demand of $500,000. I know you need much more, Christine, but unless they let it go to the jury, this is all we can demand."

Christine looked at her father, then looked back at Cephas and said, "Whatever you can do, Mr. Hampton. It will have to work."

"Cyndi," said Cephas, "please take this envelope over to Byron's room."

ooooo

In Byron Heard's room were Byron, Nathan Bishop, Dr. Thomas, and Shirley Stone. Sitting on the bed were Byron, Nathan and Ms. Stone. Dr. Thomas was standing with his back against the wall facing the door.

"I have never in my life seen such stupidity," said Ms. Stone as she looked at no one in particular. "A tenured professor gets his hat handed to him by a backwater judge who can barely spell judge. Dr. Thomas, you had better be convincing tomorrow."

She looked directly at Byron and said, "Do we *now* put Nathan on the stand? What could it hurt now?"

"It could hurt plenty," said Byron. "If we put him on the stand, it will open up an avenue for Cephas to ask about his convictions with the Sherman Antitrust Act. Cephas is looking for a way to show that money was the reason the asphalt was defective. No, Nathan will just sit there and smile the remainder of the trial." He looked directly at Dr. Thomas and said, "You, on the other hand, will be testifying tomorrow. In fact, you need to get to your room and prepare."

Without saying a word, Dr. Thomas walked to the door and left. He closed the door behind him.

"Byron, first thing Monday morning," said Shirley Stone, "I want you to sue Dr. Thomas for everything his error and omissions insurance has. I want him sued personally. I want to sue his university for allowing him to use their equipment. If possible, I want to sue the students he used to perform these so-called tests. Do you understand?"

"I understand," said Byron.

At that moment, there was a knock at the door. Byron stood up and walked toward the door, and opened it.

"Yes," he said.

"Mr. Heard, this message is for you," said Cyndi Carday as she handed him the envelope.

"Thank you," said Byron, as he opened it. He looked up to Cyndi Carday and said, "Could you wait here for a few minutes? I will have something for you to give Cephas very quickly."

"Sure," said Cyndi. "I will wait."

Byron Heard looked over at Shirley Stone and said, "They are formally asking for policy limits, $500,000. What do you want to do, Ms. Stone?"

"What have we offered, so far?" she said.

"$300,000," said Byron.

...to be made whole again.

"Raise it up to $350,000."

Byron grabbed the extra chair in the room and placed it only a few feet in front of Ms. Stone.

He sat down in the chair and said, "Ms. Stone, if we do not accept this offer of policy limits tonight, it will go to the jury tomorrow and there is no telling what the number will be if we lose."

"That's right, Byron, if we lose," she said. "I do not plan on losing. We are going to get that one juror to see it our way. I just know it. $350,000 is the offer."

"Fine," said Byron. "Have it your way."

Byron took a pen, scratched through "$500,000," and wrote out "$350,000" on the note from Cephas.

He walked to the door, opened it, and said to Cyndi, "Here you go. Please take this to Cephas."

"Yes, sir," she said.

ooooo

Cephas took the envelope from Cyndi, opened it, and read it.

"What are they thinking?" thought Cephas to himself.

"Go get a good night's sleep," Cephas said to the room. "We have work tomorrow."

ooooo

At 9:00 am, Thursday, November 12, court resumed.

"I would like to recall Dr. Thaddeus Thomas to the stand," said Byron Heard.

Dr. Thomas took his seat in the witness box. Byron asked him about the need for construction signage at the incident site. As rehearsed, Dr.

103

Thomas adamantly told the jury that signage was only needed where the work activity was taking place. When asked about the eight inch drop-off where the ambulance dropped onto the shoulder, Dr. Thomas stated with much certainty that this condition preexisted the roadway project in question, and was not the responsibility of Bishop Construction Company.

"That is all I have," said Byron to Judge Aiken.

"Do you have anything for the witness, Mr. Hampton?" said Judge Aiken.

"Yes, Your Honor," said Cephas.

Cephas stood up from his chair, and walked over to the jury box, and faced Dr. Thomas.

"Dr. Thomas, are you familiar with the Red Book that has been discussed in this courtroom?"

"Of course," said Dr. Thomas.

"Good," said Cephas. "Now tell the jury where it states that the contractor is only required to use warning signs, cones, barrels, or other devices *only* where the work is taking place."

"It does not state it that specifically," said Dr. Thomas.

"In fact," said Cephas, "it requires warning signs, cones, barrels, and other devices where needed within the limits of the contract, correct?

"It is discretionary," said Dr. Thomas.

"Discretionary," said Cephas. "Let's look at another part of the Red Book."

Cephas turned directly toward the jury and began reading from the Red Book.

"The contractor will be required without direct compensation to maintain in good condition and satisfactory of the engineer the entire section or sections of highway within the limits of the contract, for the time he first begins work until all work has been completed and accepted."

"Are you familiar with this section of the Red Book, Dr. Thomas?" said Cephas.

"I am," he said.

"Was the eight inch drop-off an example of a 'good condition' in your opinion, Dr. Thomas?" said Cephas.

"The engineer never told Bishop Construction to change it," said Dr. Thomas.

"That was not my question, Dr. Thomas," said Cephas. "But since you brought it up, did you read the deposition of Trevor Arnold?

"I did," said Dr. Thomas.

"From Mr. Arnold's deposition," said Cephas, "we have the following: Question - Did you and Mr. Bishop talk about alerting the engineer to the six inch drop-off? Answer - We talked about it, but Nathan did not want to bring it up because of the cost to repair?"

Cephas walked up to the witness box, looked into Dr. Thomas' eyes and said, "The engineer never told Bishop Construction to change the drop-off because Bishop Construction never told the engineer about the drop-off, isn't that correct, Dr. Thomas?"

"That's one way of looking at it," said Dr. Thomas, knowing there was no good answer he could provide to help his client.

"That is all I have for this witness, Your Honor," said Cephas.

"Do you have any other witnesses, Mr. Heard," said Judge Aiken.

"No, sir," said Byron.

"It is 10:30," said Judge Aiken. "We will break for lunch early and reconvene at one o'clock for closing statements. Court is adjourned until one."

ooooo

At ten minutes after one o'clock, Judge Aiken had already taken his seat at the bench. All was quite in the courtroom with the exception of the sound of pens writing into notebooks or on legal pads.

Judge Aiken looked at Cephas Hampton and said, "Are you ready for your closing statement, Mr. Hampton?"

"I am, Your Honor," he said.

"Very well," said Judge Aiken.

Cephas Hampton stood up from his chair, paused for a few seconds, looked over to Christine Jesup in her wheelchair to give a knowing smile, looked up toward the jury box and began speaking without moving from the table.

"Ladies and gentlemen of the jury, for the past few days, you have heard the case of the incident involving Bishop Construction Company. Nathan Bishop and his employees were hired by the South Carolina Department of Transportation to overlay Old Sheldon Church Road with asphalt, in a good, workmanlike manner. They were hired to place a quality asphalt in a manner that did not compromise the safety of the public after the job was complete, or when the Bishop Construction Company had control of the roadway work area. It is without question that Bishop Construction Company had control of the roadway work area when the ambulance carrying Dr. Christine Jesup fell down the eight inch drop-off, and crashed into that oak tree. It is without question that Dr. Christine Jesup injured her spine as a result of that crash on Old Sheldon Church Road when it was in the control of Bishop Construction Company. What is in question, ladies and gentlemen of the jury, is whether or not the actions, or as has been presented, the inactions, of Bishop Construction Company were the cause of the ambulance crash."

Cephas walked from behind the table and spoke as he walked toward the jury box.

"My friends," he said, "you have everything you need to render judgment in this matter. You have the contract documents signed by Bishop Construction Company. You have the Red Book that clearly outlining the responsibilities of Bishop Construction Company regarding asphalt specifications and safety signage. You have the expert witness testimony of Allen Sterling who, by comparison to the other expert witness, actually knows a thing or two about how to design and build roads."

There was a slight rustling heard from the jury box. Several of the jurors had slight grins and nodded in agreement.

"And there's one more thing," said Cephas. "You have Dr. Christine

Jesup. A woman who, at the prime of her life, was made a quadriplegic. Who no longer has the ability to save lives, deliver babies, or to make us well. Dr. Christine Jesup needs help to make us well, again."

Cephas paused for a few seconds, placed his hands on the jury box rail in front of the jurors and said, "On behalf of Dr. Christine Jesup and her family, I respectfully request that all of you good people find in her favor. I respectfully request that you compensate Dr. Jesup with a monetary sum that will pay for her long term care; that will provide some comfort for those long periods of rehabilitation; and to show others who do business in Beaufort County that we will not tolerate self-serving interpretations of contracts, and shoddy work."

Cephas paused, looked down at the rail, and then his gaze returned to the jurors. He said, "We need Dr. Christine Jesup to make us well, again. She needs your help…to be made whole again."

Cephas stepped back two steps and said, "Thank you."

Judge Aiken looked and Byron and said, "You may begin, Mr. Heard." "Thank you, Your Honor," said Byron.

Byron stood up, walked out in front of his table, and began speaking to the jury. He never left that spot.

"Interesting words from Mr. Hampton, I must admit ladies and gentlemen," he said with a slight sarcastic tone. "We do not dispute that an *accident* occurred on Old Sheldon Church Road, and that injuries occurred. What we dispute is that Bishop Construction Company is responsible when Nathan Bishop and his employees were miles away, doing their jobs as directed by the SCDOT, when the accident occurred. They were nowhere near it!"

He paused for a few seconds.

"Interesting words, indeed," he said. "Three words that come to mind are self…serving…interpretations. Just who is actually using self-serving interpretations here? Mr. Hampton would have you believe that his expert's interpretations, or opinions if you will, are as pure as the wind-driven snow. But what Mr. Hampton conveniently wants you to forget is that a tenured professor, Dr. Thaddeus Thomas, does not agree with Mr. Sterling. Dr. Thomas's opinions – his interpretations – are sound and are backed by decades of experience."

Byron started walking toward the jury box. Like Cephas had done a few minutes earlier, and in a mocking fashion, Byron placed in hands on the jury box rail.

"On behalf of Nathan Bishop, the employees of Bishop Construction Company who rely on its jobs, and on behalf of all the people who rely on businesses like those run by Nathan Bishop, please see this as the unfortunate accident – not incident – but accident, that it was. Please do the right thing and find in favor of the defense. Thank you."

Byron nodded his head toward the jury, turned and walked back to his table.

"Ladies and gentlemen of the jury, it is three o'clock." said Judge Aiken. "For the remainder of the day, I will read to you your instructions. Afterwards, you will begin deliberations. Please deliberate until five o'clock. Please be back in the jury deliberation room at nine o'clock tomorrow morning to continue your deliberations."

For the next thirty minutes, Judge Aiken read the jurors' instructions. As part of those instructions, he emphasized the wisdom of immediately selecting a jury foreman or forewoman. They were to go over all the evidence heard, consider the validity of each piece of evidence, and then begin voting. Only when there was a unanimous decision could there be a verdict.

Sally Flournoy was elected by the jurors to be the jury forewoman. Dr. Jesup had delivered Sally's youngest, a daughter. As a mother of four, with three of them being older boys, she was seen as a natural to control a room should things get contentious.

...to be made whole again.

ooooo

"I think you pulled a rabbit out of the hat," said Shirley Stone to Byron Heard and Nathan Bishop in Byron's motel room. Byron was sitting on his bed with his back against the headboard. Ms. Stone was sitting in the desk chair. Nathan Bishop was standing next to the door between the door and the window. "You showed them exactly what this was; an accident."

Byron was not so sure. Yes, he had a tenured professor provide contradictory opinions regarding safety signage. But the jury had seen that tenured professor be denied his opportunity to testify about the asphalt pavement. That hurt, badly. Byron sat there quietly and listened as Nathan and Ms. Stone compared what they had seen in the courtroom. After a few minutes, there was a knock at the door.

Nathan Bishop opened the door and said, "Yes?"
"This is from Cephas Hampton to Byron Heard," said Cyndi Carday, as she handed the note to Nathan Bishop.

Without saying a word, Nathan closed the door, turned and walked over to Byron, who opened the note and read it.

"Well, here is their final demand," said Byron. "Four million dollars."
"Those arrogant people," said Ms. Stone. "Do they not know when they are beaten?"

Byron sat there and did not speak while Ms. Stone and Nathan offered reason after reason why this was just an accident; why the evidence supported their position; and why Cephas and Dr. Jesup were only trying to take money from a deep pocket insurance company.

After a few minutes of listening and thinking, Byron said, "Have either of you heard the phrase, 'you can't fight home cooking?'"
"No," said Ms. Stone. "It does sound like something created in the South."
"It is a phrase, and yes, a southern phrase," said Byron pointedly

toward Ms. Stone, "It means you cannot fight an opponent with too much of a home field advantage. Let's lay it out. You are in court in the county were Dr. Jesup lives. You have jurors who know Dr. Jesup because she delivered their babies, or are relatives of those who had the babies. You have a judge that barely allowed our expert to testify. And you have Dr. Jesup herself. Her injuries are severe, and will take a long time to heal, if at all. That, my friends, is a lot of home cooking."

"Even if they jury gets it completely wrong, those things you mentioned are grounds for appeal, correct?" said Ms. Stone.

"They could be," said Byron. He sat there quietly for a few seconds. "Ms. Stone, as your counsel, I strongly recommend that we counteroffer with at least two million to make this go away. Even if we appeal, we could lose and you would owe much more."

Ms. Stone sat in the desk chair staring intently at Byron while he spoke. She spun the desk chair around and grabbed a notepad and a pen. She wrote a number on the notepad, tore it off the pad, and handed it directly to Nathan, who was still standing by the door. Whether she meant it or not, this was an insult to Byron. She was openly bypassing him by giving the note directly to Nathan.

"They want four million," said Ms. Stone. "They can have four hundred thousand."

Byron grinned at her. He looked toward Nathan who was waiting like a puppy for his next command. Byron nodded his head toward Nathan, who turned, went out the door, and walked the note over to Cephas' room.

ooooo

Cephas read the note. "Tomorrow is going to be an interesting day," he said to Cyndi Carday and Bill Buttermore, as he took a drink of bourbon.

16 – THE VERDICT

In the hallway outside the courtroom were two camps. At one end of the hallway was the camp that consisted of Cephas Hampton, Dr. Christine Jesup, her father, Allen Sterling, Dr. Maurice Honeycutt, Cyndi Carday, and Bill Buttermore. At the other end of the hallway was the other camp, consisting of Byron Heard, Shirley Stone, and Nathan Bishop. Each camp had been in the hallway since nine o'clock, when the jury began the day's deliberations. It was Friday, November 13, at 10:50 am.

"Do you think they will get this finished today?" Ms. Stone asked Byron.

"I have no idea," he said. "Odds are it will be after lunch."

"I hope it is not too late after lunch," she said. "I have a plane to catch by six pm."

ooooo

"Did we do the right thing, Cephas?" said Christine with a scared tone in her voice. "I mean, four hundred thousand is a lot of money. It could help."

"Christine," he said, as he grabbed her hand, looked up at her father, and then back down to her, "you heard the other doctors. You heard Dr. Honeycutt. Four hundred thousand will only help you so much. It will only go so far. Yes, it will prolong your life; but only for a few years at most. You need the kind of money that will see you walk again; the kind of money that will allow you to deliver babies again. That is what you want, isn't it, Christine?"

She firmed up her lips, and with the loudest sound she had made in months, she said, "Yes!"

"Good," he said.

Cephas stood up and started to walk toward the other camp at the other end of the hallway. Byron stood up from his chair to greet him. Ms. Stone and Nathan kept their seats, each with a slight grin on their faces.

"So, are you ready to settle, Cephas?" said Byron almost knowing what the answer was going to be.

"Yes, Byron," said Cephas. "The number is still four million dollars."

At that moment, Ms. Stone stood up in a huff, looked at Cephas and said, "Quit wasting my time."

"Well, there you have it, Cephas," said Byron.

For the first time in this case, Cephas realized who had been calling the shots. Byron was only doing the bidding of his client.

"I finally understand," said Cephas. He gave a knowing grin to Byron as he turned and walked away back toward his camp. Just as Cephas reached his people, the bailiff Floyd Tarpley opened the courtroom door, and stepped into the hall.

"The verdict is in," said Floyd Tarpley.

"The jury only deliberated for four hours," said Christine. "Is this good?"

"I'm not sure, Christine," said Cephas. "I'm not sure."

ooooo

By 11:15 am, everyone had taken their seats in the courtroom of Judge Aiken.

"All rise," said Floyd Tarpley. While everyone who could came to their feet, Judge Aiken walked from the entrance to his chambers to his chair at the bench.

"Please take your seats," said Judge Aiken.

After a few moments of noise as the people sat down, Judge Aiken picked up the folder in front of him and said, "We are here for the matter of Dr. Christine Jesup v. Bishop Construction Company. He looked toward jurist Sally Flournoy and said, "Madam Forewoman, have you reached a verdict?"

"We have, Your Honor," she said.

"And how do you find?" said Judge Aiken.

"We find for the plaintiff, Your Honor."

With that news, Cephas Hampton's back straightened, and Byron Heard's face dropped.

"And for what amount, Madam Forewoman?" said Judge Aiken.

"Ten million dollars in damages, Your Honor," said Sally.

Cephas immediately looked at Christine. Her eyes were filled with tears. Her father was crying and smiling at the same time as he put his arm around his daughter. Judge Aiken made some closing remarks to thank the jury for their service, and maybe something else. Cephas was deaf with disbelief. Afterwards, Judge Aiken banged the gavel, and court was adjourned.

Cephas stood up, turned around, and saw Dr. Maurice Honeycutt standing nearby with a look of relief and pride on his face. He extended his hand toward Cephas.

As they shook hands, Dr. Honeycutt said, "You did good today, Cephas. You did good."

"You're welcome, Cuz," he said.

Cephas looked around the courtroom where things were getting loud. It was obvious that a majority of the people here were in favor of the verdict.

Byron Heard was still sitting in his chair with his face turned down toward the desk while the uproar continued in the courtroom.

Shirley Stone had a look of disbelief on her face. Without looking directly at anyone, she said, "Now what do we do?"

Byron raised his head, turned it quickly toward her, and said, "Negotiation or appeal, Ms. Stone. The choice is yours. And I promise you the negotiation will start a lot higher than four hundred thousand dollars."

The End

Richard A. Rice, PE

A NOTE FROM THE AUTHOR

Thank you for taking the time to read "*...to be made whole again.*" This is my first book. I hope you have found it to be as entertaining and informative as I have found it to be a pleasure to write.

Working as a forensic engineer on roadway incidents, building collapses, construction accidents, and other types of civil/structural engineering cases is an honor and a privilege. It is the coolest job in the world. I wish the same for you.

Sincerely,

Richard

Made in the USA
Middletown, DE
08 December 2014